SH

A fusillade o ...
halted in their tracks. Instantly the r...
furious fire, but the damage was done. The Indians were
hard to see; they lay in sandy ruts, loading and firing, a
hundred yards away.

Monk swore, ducking as sniping shots cracked near him.
Ki yelled at the others to fire at the muzzle flashes. Jessie
lay in one of the third-rank wagons and fired at flashes,
several times seeing a hand or a leg thrown up, signs
of a hit.

The riflemen spread along the ground, crawling forward,
firing, and crawling again.

At once the Sioux fire diminished . . .

* * *

SPECIAL PREVIEW

Turn to the back of this book for an exciting look
at a new epic trilogy . . .

Northwest Destiny

. . . the sprawling saga of brotherhood, pride and
rage on the American frontier.

DON'T MISS THESE
ALL-ACTION WESTERN SERIES FROM
THE BERKLEY PUBLISHING GROUP

THE GUNSMITH by J. R. Roberts
Clint Adams was a legend among lawmen, outlaws, and ladies. They called him . . . the Gunsmith.

LONGARM by Tabor Evans
The popular long-running series about U.S. Deputy Marshal Long—his life, his loves, his fight for justice.

LONE STAR by Wesley Ellis
The blazing adventures of Jessica Starbuck and the martial arts master, Ki. Over eight million copies in print.

SLOCUM by Jake Logan
Today's longest-running action western. John Slocum rides a deadly trail of hot blood and cold steel.

WESLEY ELLIS

LONE STAR

AND THE GUNRUNNERS

JOVE BOOKS, NEW YORK

LONE STAR AND THE GUNRUNNERS

A Jove Book / published by arrangement with
the author

PRINTING HISTORY
Jove edition / September 1992

ISBN: 0-515-10930-4

Jove Books are published by The Berkley Publishing Group,
200 Madison Avenue, New York, New York 10016.
The name "JOVE" and the "J" logo
are trademarks belonging to Jove Publications, Inc.

PRINTED IN THE UNITED STATES OF AMERICA

10 9 8 7 6 5 4 3 2 1

★

Chapter 1

The U.S. Army Armory at Hitchens comprised a red brick administration building, which also housed officers' quarters, a large warehouse divided into compartments and workshops, a stable and various sheds, and an enlisted men's barracks, mostly empty, there being only a handful of men on the post.

The armory had been built and operated during the late war, but its functions were now no longer needed since the large center at Leavenworth was easily able to supply the army's fewer requirements.

Rumors were rife that Congress would abolish the Hitchens Arsenal at the next session, cause the equipment and stores to be moved, and sell the land and buildings.

The armory was surrounded by a high wire fence. It had several gates, and the one to the warehouse was very wide, to accomodate large wagons and wains. All gates were chained and locked at night and no guard was mounted.

An hour after midnight on Saturday, a buckboard pulled by a single horse, with five men aboard, came down the road from town and halted by the wide gate.

Esek Kite cut a large enough hole in the wire fence to allow the wagon to drive through.

His partner, Preacher Hanks, sat beside the driver, a shotgun across his knees. The two had hired three toughs, known to them only as Joe, Henry, and Tex, to help with the job. Joe was an expert with locks. He jumped down and opened the warehouse door, and Tex drove the wagon inside. Esek struck a match and lighted a lantern.

According to the information they had bought from an enlisted man who worked there, the warehouse stored a hundred or more crates of Spencer rifles, carbines, and ammunition. These would bring a goodly amount in the proper places; Spencers were in demand. It was an eight-shot rifle, seven in the magazine and one in the chamber, and had proved its worth in the war.

Once inside the warehouse, they spread out at Preacher's order, looking for the crates.

They did not find them.

Instead they found two dozen crates containing old single-shot 1861 rifled muskets made at the Springfield Armory.

Preacher kicked the boxes, growling. "We been diddled! These things ain't worth a damn."

"There ain't no Spencers here," Esek said. "This place been cleaned out. You figger we can sell these?"

Preacher sighed. "No sense goin' out empty-handed. Put a couple on board. We'll git us a few dollars for 'em."

They loaded two crates into the buckboard and turned the wagon around. At that moment a voice called out, "What you doin' in there?"

"Put out the goddam lights," Preacher snapped. The man in the doorway struck a match. Preacher lifted the shotgun and fired. The figure in the doorway was hurled aside.

The hired men scrambled aboard the wagon and Esek slapped the reins. "Hit the collar!" They raced for the door and as they rolled through it, someone off to the right fired at them with a pistol.

Esek had to slow to go through the hole cut in the wire, and the man fired again three times. Preacher turned the shotgun on him and Tex fired with a pistol. Henry coughed and slid off the wagon, rolling and floundering for a few seconds.

Esek galloped the horse into the dark. In the back, Joe said, "We lost Henry . . ."

Preacher reloaded the shotgun. "He dead, you figger?"

"Probably."

2

Esek pulled up at the edge of town. "Anybody else hit?"

No one had been. There were two holes in the wagon, and they were lucky the horse was untouched, but it was a bum trip, all in all.

Tex said, "Me 'n' Joe, we'll git off here. You pay us now, Preacher."

Preacher slapped a few dollars into his hand.

"This ain't what you promised us!"

"That's all we got. B'sides, we didn't git them Spencers. You take it or leave it." He had the shotgun handy.

Tex looked at the twin muzzles and jumped off the wagon. Joe followed, screwing up his face, but neither wanted to tangle with Preacher.

"You all keep your mouths shut," Preacher warned.

Esek slapped the reins and they moved on.

Preacher Chaney Hanks was a tall, stooped man with narrow shoulders and a nearly perpetual sour expression on his usually unshaven face. He often looked as if he smelled something bad; it might have been himself.

He was forty-two, with scraggly brown hair and a long, limp mustache that always needed trimming. He customarily wore black clothes of the cheapest variety, and when he cadged drinks in a saloon, he quoted the Old Testament. He was fond of giving impromptu sermons in deadfalls, and he never missed passing the hat. "Thankee, peace, brother."

He was not a preacher and had never studied to be one. Long ago, as a joke, someone had called him "Preacher," and he had quickly invested himself with the title, though the Lord must have shuddered to hear it.

His abiding passion was a deep hatred of organized society in general. Abandoned by his parents at an early age, he had been reared in various uncaring homes and before he was seven had been put to work in the fields from dawn to dusk. He had never seen the inside of a school. Much later he had learned to write his name, but little else. He carried

3

a Bible for effect when he was with folks among whom he could pass the hat. He learned not to gaze at the book when it was upside down. In a few years, in his late teens, he had perfected the masquerade to such an extent that no one questioned him. He was not a stupid man and he did not find it difficult to collect a crowd that would listen to his ravings. People loved a good fire-and-brimstone sermon, and loved for him to rant about certain sins, especially those between men and willing women. When he got down to details, his hat always reflected the extent when it was passed. The more lurid, the better the take.

Then one day, after one of his sermons, a man came to see him at his hotel. Esek Kite was a shorter, rather dumpy-looking man, an ex–mule skinner. He had a round face, toothy and squinty eyed, and black hair, and he confessed to Preacher that he'd been out of jail less than a month. He suggested that they both needed a partner. "You as big a thief as me."

Preacher growled, but he knew instinctively that Esek knew him for what he was. He had never made another friend in the world, but in the days that followed, he and Esek got along famously. They were quite different, but the same. "Birds of a feather," Esek said.

They were run out of a dozen towns but always managed to make a living; there were lean times and good . . . Some communities were receptive to Preacher's fiery sermons, others not. If not, they broke into stores or held up travelers, but they never got far ahead of the game; they eked out a living, but were always looking for the big score.

When they came to a town, their first act was to make the rounds of the saloons. If a crowd seemed receptive, Preacher would give a sermon. A hush would always fall on the saloon as he described the sin of bedding women of easy virtue: how to take off a woman's clothes—his listeners strained to catch every word—and lay her on a bed.

He never bothered with small sins because his audiences had always grown restless when he'd tried, years ago.

4

Preacher and Esek had been camped on the road to Hitchens when Esek mentioned that he had, quite by chance, listened to a conversation he found fascinating. Some men had talked about selling spirits and guns to Indians. It was a business, the men said, with damned little competition. It required guts.

Preacher asked, "You figger Indians got any money to pay?"

"They got loot from raiding, don't they?"

"Umm. Well how we reach any Indians so we can trade?"

"Drive out on the prairie, I reckon. We got us a light wagon."

"What if they start shooting?"

Esek shrugged. "You take a chance. Hell, we been taking chances for years."

Preacher nodded. Of course mostly they'd been dodging the law. Could you outrun a bunch of Indians? Esek thought they could try.

They had few dollars between them, not enough to buy guns for resale, but enough for several kegs of whisky. At a creek they made six kegs from three; then they bought a few tin cups and drove far out onto the prairie.

They learned very quickly it was not a good policy to sell liquor by the cup. Indians got drunk very fast and on several occasions began firing guns and demanding more whiskey without payment.

So they sold entire kegs, took what payment they could get, and drove off before the firewater took effect.

In this manner they learned a few words of the Sioux language and learned about Running Wolf, a war leader. The red man came to see them. He was able to speak passable English because he'd been reared in a missionary settlement until the age of ten. He was a big, burly man, arrogant and disdainful of whites, but greedy for firearms and powder.

"You bring guns. I buy."

Preacher nodded. "How many guns?"

"I buy all you bring. Powder and lead too."

"Can you pay?"

The Indian's eyes flashed. He had lived among whites and knew how they prized gold. Money meant nothing to him; only guns spoke his tongue. He tossed them a few gold pieces. "You bring guns."

Esek grinned, fingering the gold eagles. "All right. Where?"

"You know Bear Rock?"

"Yes . . ."

"We meet there. You bring guns one week."

"It ain't goin' to be easy to get guns," Preacher said. "We'll need more time. Two weeks anyway."

Running Wolf regarded them unblinkingly and finally nodded.

When they went back to town, Preacher mentioned Hitchens. "The armory ought to be easy . . ."

"Maybe."

Then they met Billy Larson in a saloon. Billy was an enlisted man stationed for the moment at the Hitchens Arsenal. The arsenal held hundreds of cases of Spencers, he told them, when Esek crossed his palm with gold and promised him more.

There was no guard mounted, Billy said, the fence was thought to be enough. He told them exactly how to cut the fence and open the warehouse.

They gave him all the gold and money they had.

★

Chapter 2

Jessica Starbuck and Ki went to Hitchens as soon as they heard that Colonel Edmund Dakins had died from wounds suffered when the arsenal was robbed. Dakins was a long-time friend of her father's, and a general officer in the war.

Jessie stepped down from the stagecoach, and every man within eyesight stopped in his tracks and stared. No one in Hitchens had seen such a vision, a honey-blond, green-eyed beauty in blue jeans and a white blouse. She walked to the hotel across the wide street, breasts bobbing as heads swiveled and some forgot to breathe.

No one noticed the man who followed her, tall and dark, wearing black jeans, a loose cotton shirt, and a black leather vest. He might have been an Indian, or an Oriental, or perhaps a Mexican—if anyone had been able to tear his gaze from the incredible vision that entered the hotel.

Everyone sighed and took long breaths—and tried to remember what he had been doing when the door of the stagecoach had opened.

The same day Ki obtained two horses from the livery, and he and Jessie rode to the arsenal. The officer in charge was Captain Willard Banes, who greeted them gravely. He had received a wire from Washington, he told them, directing him to offer Miss Starbuck every courtesy and assistance.

"I am told your father and Colonel Dakins were close, and I am truly sorry to greet you under such circumstances . . ."

"Thank you, Captain."

7

Colonel Dakins's body had already been shipped east, Banes explained, at the request of his wife and family. "And the enlisted man who was killed was buried in the local cemetery several days ago."

"Tell us, if you will, just how the robbery took place and how the men were killed."

"Certainly. If you will come this way to the warehouse . . ." He took them from the brick building into the cavernous warehouse, pointing out where the wagon had come through the cut wire fence and where men had removed several crates of rifles.

"The robbers took with them two crates of '61 model Springfields. I can't imagine they came for them. Nobody wants single-shot arms any longer. But at any rate they took two boxes." He pointed to a row of crates. "They could have taken half a dozen."

Ki said, "That suggests, sir, that they came for something else, doesn't it, and were disappointed?"

"Yes. I certainly agree. As you can see our shelves are about empty." Captain Banes moved his hand about. "In another month nothing will remain here at all. I have orders to ship everything to Leavenworth. The army will probably appoint a caretaker for the premises and all of us will be gone too."

Jessie asked, "How was Colonel Dakins killed?"

"We found Private Boggs's body there by the door. He had been hit by a shotgun blast. We assume that he stumbled upon the robbers and they shot him. He died instantly. They then came out of the warehouse and were seen by Colonel Dakins."

Captain Banes led them to the open door. "The colonel was badly wounded and I was able to talk to him at the hospital before he died. He told me he had come from the office and was enjoying a cigar when he heard the shot. He immediately ran toward the warehouse and was drawing his pistol when the wagon, a light buckboard, came out and made for the hole in the wire. Colonel Dakins fired

8

three or four shots and was hit and fell. One of the men on the wagon was also hit and died very shortly. He was not identified."

"What in the world was Colonel Dakins doing here?" Jessie asked.

Banes smiled. "He was on an inspection tour. Part of his duty was probably to report that this arsenal is no longer needed."

Ki asked, "Where were you, sir?"

"I was in Bicker, visiting friends who were getting married. That's about forty miles south of here. While there I received a wire saying Colonel Dakins was arriving, and I immediately returned. I got here the day after the shooting."

Jessie said, "May we question the men who are here?"

"Certainly. We have several empty offices. I'll arrange it at once."

"Thank you."

Banes said grimly, "I want to see those men brought to justice as well as you do." He paused. "By the way, one of my men has disappeared."

"Disappeared?"

"There are nine enlisted men quartered here at the arsenal. Two mornings ago at roll call, only eight showed up. I sent my sergeant into town to see if the missing man happened to be in the town jail, drunk. He was not."

His name was Billy Larson.

When they questioned the eight enlisted men, one by one, they found that Private Hack Strehl had been a close friend of the missing man.

Jessie asked him, "Do you know where Larson went?"

"No idea, ma'am."

"He gave no hints before leaving?"

"No, nothin' at all." Strehl shrugged. "It don't make sense, him leaving now."

"Why not?"

"Because his hitch was almost up. Time we got moved to Leavenworth, he'd be out of the army . . . or close to it. And he had a girl in Leavenworth he was writin' to. I seen the letters."

When Strehl had gone, Ki asked, "Is there any chance, do you think, that Larson went with the robbers?"

"That's an interesting idea," Jessie said. "Or maybe they took him prisoner."

"Why would they do that?"

She smiled. "No idea. But maybe he knew something they wanted."

Ki said, "It would make more sense, wouldn't it, that Larson knew something they wanted *before* the robbery? Maybe how to get into the armory?"

Jessie snapped her fingers, "Or information about what was *in* it!"

"But there's nothing much in it."

"The robbers wouldn't know that."

Ki laughed. "You mean they paid Larson for information—and he lied to them?"

She nodded. "Maybe that's why he's missing."

The body of Private Billy Larson was brought into town that afternoon and taken to the undertaker's office. Jessie and Ki were notified by the town marshal and met him there.

The body was laid out on a metal table and the undertaker, a slim middle-aged man named Booth, informed them that the young soldier had died of a gunshot wound to the chest.

"It went right through the ticker, gents and Miss. I'd say he was shot from about three feet away."

Jessie asked, "Where was the body found?"

"Out on the prairie, maybe three miles from town," the marshal said. "I talked to old man Netter, who found 'im. Netter was out looking for some strays when he seen the buzzards and come across the body, facedown in the grass."

"How long ago was he shot?" Jessie asked.

"Rigor's past," Booth said. "Maybe three days. Two or three days ago. There ain't a thing on him either. No money, no pocket knife, no tobacco, not nothing."

"Is that unusual?"

"Sure is. Somebody stripped him."

When they had gone back to the hotel, Jessie said, "Why don't we talk to Private Strehl again . . . ?"

"You have an idea?"

"I'm wondering why there was nothing in Larson's pockets."

"He was robbed."

"Yes—of what?"

He was robbed of a silver watch, Strehl told them. "It was a watch his pa give him. Damn fine timepiece. He was proud of it. I guess it was the best thing he owned."

"Was his name on it?"

"Oh yes. On the inside, engraved."

"The killer took it," Jessie said. "Now all we have to do is . . ."

★

Chapter 3

When they had dropped off Joe and Tex, they made a swing around the town and camped by a stream, to sleep under the wagon. Esek made a fire and boiled coffee while Preacher pulled a 'paulin over the crates and tied it down firmly.

Esek said, "You figger that Indian, Runnin' Wolf, will buy these here single shooters?"

"Why not? They's guns, ain't they?"

"Yeah. Course he didn't say what kind of guns he wants. How smart is that Injun, anyway?"

Preacher shrugged. "If he buys these, maybe we can sell him more."

"If he's got more gold."

"That's right. We can pick up rifles here and there, maybe make us some good kale." He sipped the coffee. "What we need is a house."

"What for?"

"So we can hide the guns. We can't go runnin' around the damn landscape with a wagon loaded down with guns. If somebody stops us—the law or soldiers—we'd be in the soup. We need some place to keep 'em. If that Indian will buy all the shooters we bring him, we got a good business here."

It was no trick to find Billy Larson in town. He was drinking with two others from the arsenal, in the White Owl Saloon.

They waited patiently till he came out, alone, stumbling a little and surprised to see them. "What you want?"

12

Esek put a pistol in his back and Preacher pulled him by the blouse. "You comin' along with us."

"Where we goin'?"

"Just for a little walk. We got somebody f'you to meet."

"Who?"

Preacher got him moving. "You'll see."

They walked him out onto the prairie, Larson stumbling and tripping over clods and clumps of grass. He moaned and swore with every step. "Why can't we meet whoever it is in town?"

"Shut up and keep walkin'."

After the first mile Larson got stubborn and Esek had to whack him with the pistol barrel to keep him moving. He tried to run and fell down. Preacher picked him up and they went on. It was an overcast night with no stars and a slight chill in the air.

In a coulee, Preacher halted. "This's good enough."

Larson looked around blearily. "They nobody here." He stared at Esek as the stocky man cocked his pistol. "What the hell you doing?"

Esek smiled. "This is who you're meeting, Billy. You lied to us about them Spencers."

Larson yelled. "I thought they was in the warehouse!"

"The hell you did," Esek said, and pulled the trigger.

They needed a house on the edge of town, they decided, a place where prying eyes would not annoy them by bringing the law to ask embarrassing questions. In order to trade with the roving Indians, they had to drive out onto the grass. The spot Running Wolf had mentioned, Bear Rock, was many miles away, so they might be gone for days at a time. It was important they find a place where they could come and go without being noticed.

And they found it—a stout cabin on the road to the next town, Logan, well outside of Leavenworth. It was a long-established road, well rutted and seldom traveled, ideal for their purposes. One could turn off it at any point with

13

a wagon; there were no fences. The vast prairie stretched from their front door into the distance.

But no one had lived in the cabin for years. They spent days swabbing it out to make it livable. It was well off the road, under some scraggly cottonwoods, and had a small parlor, large kitchen with a pump, two tiny bedchambers, and a wide porch, where wood was ricked up out of the weather.

Also on the property was a three-stall stable, once whitewashed, and a mostly falling-down fence that surrounded the buildings. The entire shebang belonged to a merchant in town who was delighted that someone wanted to pay him rent for it.

When they drove the buckboard to Bear Rock two weeks later, Running Wolf was already there with several other braves. The Indians inspected the Springfields, jabbered among themselves, grunting and gesturing, and finally Running Wolf agreed to take them but said he wanted fast-shooting guns.

"Boom, boom, boom," he said, simulating lever-action rifles.

Preacher took the gold he offered and promised to get them.

Jessie and Ki sat in her hotel room, discussing the case. It was beginning to look difficult. There were no live witnesses to the shooting at the armory or the murder of Larson on the prairie.

At least three men had driven a light wagon into the warehouse, loaded two crates of rifles, and killed two men in the process.

Captain Banes told them that in his only talk with the dying Colonel Dakins, Dakins had said he'd seen several men on the wagon, probably four, but it had been too dark to get a good look. He could not describe them.

But that was more than they'd known before. They were looking for at least three men.

14

Ki said, "They got away with old guns. They only took two crates when they could have had five or six. That means they knew the guns weren't worth much. Each man would get only a few dollars. I agree with the Larson theory now . . . that Billy Larson lied to them for the money they would pay him."

"It does make sense that way. So they took Billy out away from town to execute him."

Ki nodded. "Would an ordinary holdup man take his victim two miles out of town to rob him? Not likely."

"I think you're right."

"But there's one other question. Did the gang stay together? They might have gone in four directions by now."

Jessie sighed. "Yes, that's possible too. We ought to find where they sold those muskets."

It did not prove to be easy. They looked into every gun shop and gunsmith in Leavenworth and the surrounding towns. No one had bought a cache of Springfield rifles, not even a single piece.

Ki growled about it. "Why would they take the guns if not to sell them?"

"The Big Muddy isn't far. Maybe they sold them to someone who took them up or down river." She sighed. "And if so, they may be gone forever."

Ki agreed glumly. That was a very real possibility.

And then they had a piece of luck. While they were asking about men selling Springfields, they were told about two men who were buying rifles.

A gunsmith in Leavenworth said, "I ain't bought no Springfields lately because nobody wants 'em. They all big, long buggers, they weigh a ton and they's single shooters. As far's guns go, they damn good if you got a fort. Most folks hasn't."

Jessie said, "You mentioned that two men were buying rifles? More than one rifle?"

"Yep. Bought some Winchesters."

"Some? Why would someone want several rifles?"

15

The gunsmith made a face. "Maybe to sell 'em to some-body else?"

"What did the two men look like?"

The gunsmith pursed his lips. "One was a big, stooped gent and the other'n was short and stocky. The big one did all the talkin'."

"And you sold them several rifles?"

"I sold 'em four and they paid with gold eagles. Said they was buying for a wagon train. Bought ammunition too. Took it all out and put 'em in a buckboard."

"For a wagon train?"

"Yep. They's still folks movin' west."

Jessie smiled and thanked him.

As they were leaving the shop the gunsmith said, "One more thing . . ."

"What?"

"The short one called the other'n Preacher."

They bought repeating rifles and ammunition everywhere they could, using the same excuse: they were buying for a wagon train. Nobody questioned that. Now and then they were able to buy a Spencer, but it took special ammunition. The Winchesters and Colt pistols used the same ammo.

They quickly used up their capital—and needed more guns.

Preacher said, "We got to get guns some other way."

"What other way? You mean steal 'em?"

"If we have to."

Esek was willing. "But where? Gun shops is hard to break into. They locks them sombitches up tight."

"Well, we got to get 'em . . . I dunno where." Preacher's voice rose sharply. "But if we go round pickin' up a rifle here and there it'll take us a year t'get a wagon load. And that goddam Injun ain't gonna wait no year!"

Esek nodded. That was so. "But they ain't another arsenal around, outside of Leavenworth, and we ain't got a chance of gettin' in there."

"I been thinkin' one other thing too," Preacher said moodily. "We got to make it look like we's working."

"We are working for crissakes!"

"I mean at a regular job—something folks can see we's making money at. Something respectable so's nobody sniffs around. They's plenty of noses got nothing better to do than watch other folks."

Esek sighed. He hated the idea of a job. But he had to admit Preacher had a good idea. Even if they lived out of town, some picker would wonder how they bought their beans. Luckily he had a trade, learned in prison. He was a harness maker. They agreed he would go looking for piece work in town, and Preacher would do what he did best— orate and pass the hat in saloons. With those two, they ought to be able to get by.

Their big job, Preacher said, would be to placate Running Wolf. He was sure to demand more and more guns.

Later, in the hotel, as they sat over coffee, Ki said, "That gunsmith said maybe those two were selling the guns to somebody else."

"He also said they were buying them for a wagon train."

"Yes, but I doubt that."

"Why?"

"Because every family that joins a wagon train is certain to have its own guns. Why would someone buy guns for a train? It doesn't add up. It sounds good, but it doesn't make sense."

"Umm. Then what's your guess?"

"I side with the gunsmith. I think they were buying them to sell."

"What if those two men the gunsmith told us about were selling guns to Indians?"

"Why Indians?"

Ki smiled. "Because Indians can't come into town and buy them for themselves. Whites can buy all the guns they please, but Indians can only get them from smugglers—or

17

of course, take them by force."

"Very good . . . You may have hit it!"

"Well, it's a theory. Isn't there a law that says selling guns to Indians is a federal offense?"

"There may be . . ."

"If so it ought to be a lucrative business—if you have no scruples."

"Can Indians pay for guns?"

Ki shrugged. "They may have goods to trade."

A man called Preacher, the gunsmith had said. Jessie sighed deeply. How many preachers were there in the country? Maybe thousands. Men sometimes took up the Good Book to eke out a living with it when the farm failed. It was one occupation an enterprising man could go into that required no learning. All he had to have was a gift of gab.

Ki may have hit it right, that the two were selling to Indians. Jessie bought a paper on the street and took it into the hotel to read. Ki went out somewhere to look at horses.

The newspaper listed raids by the marauding Sioux. One of the war leaders prominently mentioned was a Sioux named Running Wolf. He was apparently the most colorful of the Indian leaders, and he had a large hook nose that reporters liked to describe.

The Sioux, marvelous horsemen, were attacking small parties of whites on the plains. They even had the guts to attack army wagons and ambush small patrols.

It was rumored that Running Wolf had vowed that he and his people would drive the whites back across the Missouri. That was impossible, of course, the newspaper said, but it said something about the man.

When Ki returned, Jessie showed him the paper. He said, "*If* this man, Preacher, and his friend, *are* selling guns to the Indians, then these raids are helping them."

"How do you mean?"

"I mean, if stray whites are kept off the plains, it'll be easier for the two to reach the Indians, won't it?"

"Yes, I imagine so. But by the same token it'll be harder for us to roam about looking for them."

Ki nodded and made a wry face. "Yes, if we want to keep our hair."

★

Chapter 4

They had bought sixteen rifles, which were concealed in the stable, awaiting delivery. They had less than ten dollars between them, not enough to buy food *and* rifles. Esek was beginning to wonder if the enterprise they had entered upon was too difficult.

"We ain't got the capital, Preacher. This here needs money and we's too goddam poor to feed our horses."

"It'll change," Preacher said.

"It don't show no signs of it. We're better off travelin' and picking up what we can."

"We was poor then too, dammit!"

"Then maybe the good Lord has got no plans for us outside of lettin' us scratch for our vittles."

Preacher turned his head. "You put the horse in the stable?"

"Course." Esek looked around. "You hear something?"

"Put out the light."

Esek blew out the lantern and watched Preacher open the door cautiously.

Running Wolf said, "Me here. Don't shoot."

Esek let his breath out and pulled a match off a block and scratched it. The big Indian came into the room, ebony eyes darting here and there. Esek lifted the lamp chimney and lighted the smoking wick.

Through the open door he could see half a dozen braves in the yard. The war leader had not come alone.

Preacher said, "You give us a turn, Chief."

"You got rifles?"

"We got sixteen. They in the stable."

"Why not more?"

Esek spoke firmly. "Because we ain't got no money for crissakes." He saw Preacher stare at him, but he continued. "It takes money to buy rifles and we ain't got any."

Running Wolf gazed at him without expression. "Show me rifles."

Preacher nodded. "Thisaway . . ." He led them out and across the dark yard to the stable. It was a moonless night. Esek brought the lantern and hung it on a wire by the door. He and Preacher lifted down the wrapped packs, and Running Wolf opened them as the other braves crowded around, muttering at sight of the guns.

Esek said, "Sixteen rifles."

"We doing all we can," Preacher said. "We got to be careful of the law. It don't allow us t'sell to you."

Running Wolf nodded. He motioned with his hand, and the braves wrapped the guns again and quickly went out with them.

Preacher said, "If we get caught, you don't get no guns."

The war leader handed Preacher a leather pouch. It was very heavy, and as he opened it, the glint of gold coins made Esek smile.

"Get more guns," Running Wolf said. He stalked out to the others and mounted, and the group rode off into the prairie.

Preacher watched them go. "He knows where we live. I wonder how he done that."

"Let's see that gold." Esek took the pouch and went into the house with it. Preacher put the lantern on the table, and Esek poured the gold onto the tabletop. It made a glittering pile, and they looked at each other. Esek grinned. "That goddam Indian's smarter'n I thought."

Preacher counted the haul: three hundred and sixty dollars. "That'll feed our horse."

* * *

Jessica and Ki joined an army train headed for Fort Handley. It was anyone's guess where they should start looking for the murderers of Colonel Dakins and the enlisted man, Boggs.

They had two clues—the silver watch that had been taken and the name: Preacher. And they could not be certain that the two, Preacher and his companion, were the culprits.

The local law had determined that the man killed by Colonel Dakins on the wagon was a no-good named Henry Paydras, who had a long record of petty crimes. He was not known to run with any particular bunch and had possibly been picked up for the job at the arsenal.

The fact that the two cases of Springfields had not turned up bore out Ki's guess that the two men were buying guns to sell to the Indians. And Fort Handley was in the heart of Indian country. Since they were guessing, why not guess they might find out something there?

"If not," Ki said, "we'll go somewhere else."

Fort Handley was a frontier fort, very well kept. There was no sign of slovenliness; the grounds were swept, and whitewashed stones marked out paths with neat yellow-on-black signs here and there as guides. It was a cavalry post under the command of Colonel Isaac Gresham.

His office was in the center of a long single-story log-and-wattle building that looked strong enough to turn cannon balls.

As Jessie and Ki approached the office, Colonel Gresham came out onto the porch, and his eyes widened at sight of Jessie. She dismounted and went up the steps to take his hand. "I'm Jessica Starbuck, Colonel."

"Starbuck! Of course. I knew your father—slightly, I must add, during the war. Please come in."

He took them into his spare office and Jessie introduced Ki. She explained that they were looking for two men, one of them called Preacher.

Gresham shook his head. "There's no one here on the post like that. You say they're possibly selling guns to the tribes?"

"Yes, that's our guess." She told him about the robbery and murders at Hitchens.

Gresham frowned. "I knew Dakins very well—the army's one big family in peacetime; everyone knows everyone else. Damn, I'm sorry to hear about it."

Ki asked, "Are you having constant troubles with the tribes, sir?"

"Yes, we are. They've hit wagon trains, and our patrols have brushes with them frequently. We think they're getting bolder, and we know they're getting better weapons."

"Do you know where they're getting the guns?"

"Gunrunners, I suspect, like the two men you mentioned." Gresham's fist hit the table. "If I find them I'll hang them!"

"The civilian authorities would like to catch them as well."

"Yes. I'm sure of it." Gresham sighed. "A couple of wagons can carry a lot of rifles."

"The Kansas City papers mention a certain Running Wolf," Ki said. "Have you heard of him, sir?"

"Yes, indeed. He's a Sioux and a clever leader. My people have caught glimpses of him from time to time." He smiled. "But enough of that. I expect you'll be wanting baths and supper." He rose and called to his adjutant. "Jim, come in please." He turned to them. "This is Captain Jim Eliot. He'll put you into quarters and escort you to my home this evening. You must have dinner with Mrs. Gresham and me. She would never forgive me if you did not."

"We'd be delighted, Colonel," Jessie said. She followed Eliot out of the office. Their bags were on the porch, and Ki and Eliot carried them as they walked along the boardwalk to a row of frame houses. Eliot opened the door of number 3 and they went inside. There was a sitting room, a kitchen, and two small bedchambers.

Eliot said, "This was Major Eland's quarters before he was transferred a month ago. I hope it's satisfactory . . . ?"

"It's fine, Captain." Jessie gave him her best smile. He was a tall, deeply tanned young man, probably in his middle thirties.

He said, "Then I'll knock on the door about eight but in the meantime I'll have some men bring you hot water for the tub. I believe the tub is in this room—yes, it is."

"Thank you very much," Jessie said, meaning it.

"And you, sir," Eliot said to Ki, "we have a bathhouse just along the walk there."

"Excellent."

Supper was beef, as Jessie had known it would be, served with vegetables that had doubtless been grown in someone's garden. The carrots were mostly dried out and nearly tasteless, even with butter. But the bread was very good, freshly baked and still warm; it actually had flavor. On far army posts this was all one could expect.

Gresham's wife, Beala, was much younger than he, very trim in a dark red gown. She wanted to know all the gossip from Kansas City and St. Louis, and Jessie obliged her. They received newspapers and magazines at Fort Handley about once a month. Mrs. Gresham was the only woman on the post except for a few soldiers' wives whom she could not associate with publicly.

Her questions showed how much she desired to get back to civilization, and Jessie wondered if Gresham realized it.

They stayed three days at the post. On the third day an army patrol came back escorting a wagon in which were seven survivors of an Indian attack. Three men were badly wounded and weak from loss of blood. The others were better off but tired to death. The army physician examined them and declared all would live unless infection set in. A tiny group of houses about a trading post far out on the

24

prairie had been overrun by the tribes. Five other people had been buried on the retreat.

It was only one of such raids, Colonel Gresham told Jessie and Ki. Houses and outbuildings burned, cattle and horses driven off or killed—women and children killed. Nothing remained after these raids but scars on the land. The survivors had horrible tales to tell; they had escaped, they said, by the grace of God.

Some told of the Indian leader, a big man with a hook nose.

Colonel Gresham had the latest newspapers in his office, only a month old. Jessie and Ki read them, and Ki said, "The newspapers say that Running Wolf's vowed to drive the white-eyes from the plains—and he's doing it."

"How do the newspapers know what the Sioux are thinking?" Jessie asked.

Ki smiled. "Maybe the editors made it up."

Gresham said, "We know that whites are selling them guns, but there's too much space involved. Our troops can't be everywhere of course, and it doesn't take much for a few fast wagons to hightail over the grass at night and meet with horse Indians."

Jessie said, "Only two crates of guns came from the Hitchens Armory. Where do the others come from?"

Gresham put his finger on a map tacked to the office wall. "There's hundreds of miles between Kansas City and Nowhere along the Missouri River. Gunrunners could push out from any point. They could easily bring guns upriver on a boat, unload onto wagons, and head out into the plains." He fiddled in a drawer and brought out a cigar box, offering a cigar to Ki, who refused with thanks.

Jessie said, "The paper says the Pinkertons are on the job . . ."

Gresham lit the cigar and puffed for a moment. "Yes, the Pinkertons. There's a reward too, for information. Five hundred dollars for information leading to the apprehension of gun smugglers . . . dead or alive."

"And no takers . . ."

"No, of course not." Gresham waved. "No one's on the plains. People are moving back into towns. The police and the Pinkertons are watching the towns, and we and other army posts watch the prairies . . . or try to. We're losing the battle."

Before they left the post, another wagon train came in, six wagons and twenty troopers. They had met no opposition and seen no redskins, a lieutenant said, making his report.

They had brought supplies and a few newspapers that were hot off the press, only two weeks old. The Arapahoes had moved north since the Sioux raids, and the Cherokees had gone southwest as if not wishing to be tangled in the aspirations of Running Wolf . . . or so the paper said. The Cherokees had been badly mauled in a hard fight with the army along Silver Creek the year before and were still licking their wounds, according to army scouts.

The young lieutenant reported seeing no hostiles, but that did not mean, Colonel Gresham said, that his patrol had not been observed.

"The wagons weren't attacked," Gresham said. "It isn't clear to me that an Indian can tell if a wagon is loaded with supplies or not. I mean, it might be loaded with riflemen."

The lieutenant said, "They say in Fort Carson, sir, that it's not a good idea to underestimate Running Wolf."

"I'd like to underestimate the son of a bitch six feet underground."

★

Chapter 5

Preacher Chaney Hanks made the round of the saloons in Leavenworth, listening, talking to this one and that, giving advice on every sort of question. Preacher was always ready with advice. He would accept a drink or a cigar and listen attentively to marital troubles, always answering with positive assurance, and frequently with the same advice no matter what the question.

"You got to whap her bottom, boy. That's the way to keep a woman in line. And kids too. They step over the line, you whack 'em. They got to respect you."

"Thanks, Preacher . . ."

"Peace, brother."

He quickly learned about a wagon train making up for Fort Carson. The officers warned everyone about giving out information, but mule skinners got oiled and talked to anyone who would listen. Preacher had big ears.

Of course the most interesting fact was the date of departure. Running Wolf wanted that kind of news. The fact that fifty or sixty troopers would accompany the train was not Preacher's problem.

When he was sure he had all the facts, he left town and returned to the house he and Esek had rented, arriving after dark. There was smoke coming from the chimney, so Esek was home. They had decided not to trust the stable because they were both away so often. They had a hidden cache, a mile or so from the house. Esek had said he'd go there and load up one of the two wagons they now possessed, with rifles, powder, and shot. They would leave later that night to meet Running Wolf.

Esek was standing by the back door, in the deep shadow of the house, when Preacher dismounted in the yard. Esek let down the hammer of the pistol. "Expected you b'fore dark."

Preacher grunted. "It's ten mile. Got here as soon's I could."

He stripped the saddle and bridle from the horse in the stable while Esek poured hot water into a basin by the door. Preacher washed up, smelling the stew on the stove inside. Esek loved stews and each one he made was different. This one had a tang of garlic and a lot of tomatoes.

Preacher went in and dragged a chair to the table, spooned a bowlful and began to eat, with a chunk of bread torn from the loaf. "You et already?"

"Yeah, an hour ago. You got any news?"

"They's a wagon train goin' to Fort Carson. They leave in two days."

"With a cavalry guard?"

"Umm. A full troop."

"They sendin' more soljers out to the forts, hey? That means more patrols. The plains gettin' plumb crowded with Injuns and troopers."

"But the troopers don't travel by night. I hope to hell Runnin' Wolf remembers where to meet us."

"He'll remember. He wants them guns bad." Esek lit a cigar. "I hope he got gold instead of them damn watches and jewelry."

Preacher grunted and shook his head. He had a poor opinion of Indians; they had no damned responsibility at all. An Indian would promise with all the flowery phrases he could put together—and then forget all of it. He would also fight like a devil—then suddenly abandon the fight for no apparent reason. It was clear that Indians didn't think like whites. They were frustrating people.

He said, "Runnin' Wolf is just a damn Indian, even after all his schooling. All he knows is horses and killin'. He can't think no better'n a coyote with the mange."

Esek made a face. "That could be so, but he prob'ly thinks the same about us."

"To hell with him, so long's he pays us."

"Yeah, that's the ticket. You want any more stew?"

Preacher nodded and pushed his empty bowl across the table. "What Runnin' Wolf needs is a white man to show him how to foller up a fight. He starts fine, then he tangles it all up and them young men of his gets excited about bits of pretty cloth and forgets what they's s'posed to do."

Esek laughed. "Him with a white man? He'd never do that." He spooned more stew into the bowl. "It'd bugger up his medicine."

"I know it, and that's what makes me piss green. And that's why them Sioux are gonna get their ass kicked clean off the grass one of these days. The Sioux and all the other tribes."

"Maybe." Esek looked doubtful. "The cavalry ain't got the men t'do it though. Maybe the Indians will learn."

Preacher grunted. "And maybe hossflies will teach school. You sure full of maybes, Esek." Preacher attacked the second bowl. "You got everything ready?"

"Sure. Just hook up a team." He consulted the ormolu clock on a shelf. "We ought to leave in four, five hours. Give us a little time for some shut-eye."

Preacher nodded and wiped his mouth with a sleeve. "Pretty good stew, Esek. Hell of a lot better'n that bait I had in town."

It was midnight when they hooked up the team and led the mules out of the stable. Both mules were black and at a distance of fifty feet were almost invisible. Esek had also bought paint in town and slapped a murky brown on both buckboards. Nature protected wild creatures by coloration, he said, and they could do the same.

They traveled over the sod west and north, the boxes of tightly wrapped rifles bouncing, the ammunition boxes growling as the springless wagon took the bumps and ruts. Preacher was right, Esek thought, about Running Wolf needing an experienced white soldier to show him how to follow up an attack, but it would never come to pass. He would lose too much in the eyes of his braves to allow it . . . even if he wanted such a thing. And of course Preacher knew all that.

And Indians weren't the only things Preacher railed at. He seldom had a good word to say about anyone or anything, unless there was something to gain thereby. Esek smiled in the night. Preacher was sly, and he had been born that way. He probably didn't realize that every word he said about society was an attack on it.

They were gradually accumulating a stock of valuable articles and money—trade items from Running Wolf. The war leader had begun by paying them in gold, then suddenly changed. The articles he had given them lately had been looted from whites on various raids, and many of them, such as watches, were engraved with names and sentiments. These would have to be filed off before the items could be converted into cash, a minor annoyance.

Esek and Preacher often spent hours going over the loot, filing off letters and dividing it into two parcels—arguing endlessly over values as they did so. Neither was an expert on jewelry or stones, so they went often by size or shine, and in many cases they were not at all sure which were precious stones and which were glass.

Esek, at night in bed, often thought about his portion. By his figures there was about enough now for him to live on comfortably for the rest of his days—if he didn't splurge. That would be the thing he'd have to watch himself against. The money came so easily it didn't have the value of dollars earned by labor. He had noticed that before. Easy money *went* easy! But God! He loved to spend it! He loved to spend it on high living and women! Of course that very thing had sent him to prison—and he didn't want to go there again! He'd have to stay sober . . .

He dreamed about the women. Not the old hags in the cathouses along the river, but the ones in New Orleans! Jesus! Just one more time in New Orleans! One more time with a slinky, velvety soft, ebony-eyed girl with honey lips and clinging arms. He sighed long and deep. He'd never discussed women with Preacher, not to any extent. And Preacher seldom mentioned them except in his fiery sermons. Esek often wondered where Preacher got those exciting phrases . . .

They halted every hour or so to breathe the team, and got down to stretch their legs. The stars glittered in a dark, murky sky, and the wind sighed overhead, emphasizing the loneliness. Esek had brought along a packet of food, slices of beef and bread. They sat on the sod, backs against a wagon wheel, and ate, washing the food down with water from canteens.

The sky was getting gray in the east when they arrived at Bear Rock. No one was there to greet them, as Preacher had predicted. "That goddam Indian, he prob'ly forgot."

Esek disagreed. "He'll show up."

They made a small fire to boil coffee, and Running Wolf appeared two hours later with twenty men at his back. The big man sat his horse for a moment, looking down at them, then nodded as a white man might and said, "Good."

He slid off the horse, and it seemed to Esek that the Indian got bigger each time he saw him. Running Wolf was thickening about the middle, and his coal-black hair glistened as if wet. His broad, swarthy forehead was lined, and there were deep lines from his nose to his mouth, but the arresting feature was his hook nose—as the reporters had fastened on, calling him the hook-nosed raider. His eyes were black, though in the morning light they seemed to have great depth and a slate-like coloring about the irises that made them cold and distant. He looked at them, Esek thought, as a rattler might look at a field mouse.

It was well known that Running Wolf hated all whites, and it had been hinted that in his background there was a compelling story of betrayal that no one knew the details of. In the matter of buying weapons, of course, the Sioux was more of a realist. He *had* to depend on whites for them, because it would take all creation and then some to acquire guns by capture alone.

And of course he wanted guns of the same caliber so that the moulding of bullets would be simplified. However, that was not easily arranged.

As the Indian dismounted, Preacher touched his hat in salute. "Howdy, Running Wolf." He raised his hand, palm outward. "Glad t'see you."

The Sioux nodded again, the eagle feathers in his hair bobbing. He looked at the wagon. "What you bring?"

"Twenny fine rifles, bullets, and some whiskey."

"You bring bullets or lead?"

"We got a little of both. You got moulds, ain't you?"

Running Wolf grunted. Moulding bullets was a tedious job for white or Indian.

Esek said, "We got mostly cartridges." He walked to the wagon and pulled back the canvas cover. The Sioux leaned in, and Esek was sure the trace of a smile flitted across his dark face.

He said, "Twenny rifles?"

"That's right," Preacher said, cutting the thongs on a tightly bound bundle. The war leader picked up a rifle and hefted it.

Esek said, "It's a Whitney. Them's damn good guns."

Running Wolf looked it over. The rifle was heavy, and the cock came back with a satisfying click-clack. He picked up another.

He ought to be pleased, Preacher thought. Esek was right; they were good guns. But you could never tell what was in an Indian's mind. They'd bought the entire caboodle from a gunsmith in Kansas City, telling the man they were traders and would take the whole lot for sale to homesteaders.

The Sioux called several others, and they pawed through the goods, examining each rifle . . . Were they looking for broken parts? They sniffed the whiskey as Preacher opened the boxes of cartridges for inspection.

They had brought five kegs of whiskey and did not mention that it had been cut from two. Possibly no Indian on the plains had ever tasted pure uncut liquor. Neither Running Wolf nor any other Indian had any way to compare what the traders brought them.

Preacher opened one keg and let Running Wolf taste it and nod quickly.

Finally the Sioux slapped the side of the wagon and said something to the other braves, and they immediately pulled leather bags off the horses as Esek spread a blanket on the grass. The braves upended the contents of the bags, piling up a cascade of jewels, watches, coins, necklaces, and other trinkets. Glass and metal gleamed in the sun.

Half of it, Preacher saw instantly, was junk.

Running Wolf seated himself on one side of the blanket, Preacher and Esek on the other. The braves stayed in the background, sitting, sleeping, or muttering among themselves. One man stood impassively behind the leader.

Preacher sorted through the pile, tossing aside the obviously worthless items. There were perhaps a dozen silver watches and chains, a few still ticking. There were gold and silver bracelets and necklaces, many with brooches, some with metal ornaments. There were rings galore, earrings and loose brooches, and many seemed, because of the tarnish, to be silver. A few items Preacher thought were real gold. There were a few dozen silver spoons and forks and a few dollars' worth of coins. There might be five or six hundred dollars' worth on the blanket, maybe more if some *were* gold.

The guns and ammo had cost them near two hundred dollars. Preacher looked at Esek and said, "How you want to trade, Running Wolf?"

The Sioux gazed at him steadily a moment, then picked up a watch. "Gold," he said.

Preacher shook his head. "It's brass. It don't weigh enough t'be gold." He had never seen a brass watch, but then he was sure the Sioux hadn't either.

Running Wolf indicated the coins. "Money."

Preacher shrugged. "Then you keep it. It ain't worth much."

The Indian said, "Guns not new. Old." He nodded toward the wagon.

Esek replied, "They ain't new, but they shoot as good as new. A good rifle lasts for years. I'd carry any of them rifles m'self, Chief."

Running Wolf's eyes rested on the blanket. He looked at Preacher as if considering.

Preacher motioned to Esek. "We talk." He got up, and they walked past the wagon and halted.

Esek said, "Trade 'im even. What the hell."

"I figger they's maybe six hunnerd on the blanket."

"Yeah, me too. Don't rile him."

"Let's not give in too damn quick. It'll make it harder next time." He poked a finger at Esek. "Make it look like we's arguin' about it."

"All right." Esek looked annoyed and brushed Preacher's finger aside. "A little play-actin', huh?"

"That's right. Is he watchin' us?"

"Yeah." Esek put his arms out as if gesturing. He shook his head and Preacher grabbed his coat. Finally Esek appeared to give in.

Preacher said, "I talked you into it. We trade even. That right?"

"Right." Esek looked glum.

Preacher said, "You ought t'go on the goddam stage. Come on, let's go back."

They went back and sat; Preacher gave the Sioux a tight smile. "All right, Running Wolf, we trade even. That right with you?"

The Indian grunted and got up. He gave a string of orders and his men jumped to obey. They lifted the goods from the wagon, distributing rifles and ammunition boxes among themselves. Esek folded up the blanket with the articles inside and laid it in the wagon bed, covering it carefully with the canvas.

Preacher faced the Sioux. "When d'we meet again? You send us word?"

Running Wolf nodded. He mounted his short-tailed pony.

Preacher stepped close. "One more thing, Chief. They's a wagon train leavin' Leavenworth for Fort Carson tomorrow morning." He saw the other's eyes dilate for a second.

"Many wagons?"

Preacher shook his head. "I don't know. I think they's supplies. They's some soljers with 'em."

Running Wolf stared at him, raised his hand, and turned the pony. In another moment the entire Sioux band was streaming away across the prairie with a dust plume rising behind them.

"Let's go home," Esek said.

★

Chapter 6

Jessie and Ki left Fort Handley with a routine patrol, led by a young shavetail. He had seventeen men, and he had been out of the Point three years.

He told Jessie, "You're the first blond woman I've seen in a year and a half." He sighed. "I suppose you hear that a lot."

"I hear it now and then." She smiled. "How far is Terrill?"

"We'll reach it about noon tomorrow if we're not opposed."

They were not opposed, and the young officer's guess was nearly correct. They caught sight of the distant buildings about one o'clock in the early afternoon.

Terrill was a collection of weathered shacks and buildings that straggled along the Sage River, which was a wide, sandy wash that had one deep-running stream, narrow enough to jump across, and half a dozen trickles of slow-moving water on either side. A trail came from the north, through the town—if it could be called a town—and wandered off south. This was a track well worn by hoofs and bare feet, an ancient Indian highway that was now used mostly by whites.

The place had no streets, only open areas. The buildings were set down in a haphazard fashion, no one had bothered to step off lots. There was plenty of land; any person could have as much as he wished. It was a system that would doubtless cause problems in the future, if the town prospered and grew. But why worry about that now?

Everyone in town, Jessie thought, came out on porches or balconies to watch the patrol approach. The lieutenant halted the men in the center of the place—seven buildings, not counting a few shacks and sheds and half a dozen gray-with-age tents. Four of the buildings housed saloons; one had a dance hall and something else. Jessie saw three floozies come out onto a balcony to stare and then call to the troopers, who grinned back at them.

The lieutenant gave orders to a sergeant, then came to Jessie and Ki. "We'll be going on in half an hour," he said. "I assume you're staying here?"

"For the time being," Ki answered. "Thanks for your protection."

"Yes, thanks," Jessie said.

The officer saluted and returned to the men, who were crowding into the saloons.

Ki said, "You want to stay overnight?"

"We ought to ask about the man, Preacher."

"All right. I'll see if we can get rooms." He went into the nearest saloon as she seated herself on one of the chairs in front of it.

The saloon was called Rhomer's. It was a large room with whitewashed walls and a board floor that echoed Ki's heels. It smelled of tobacco and lamp oil. Tables cluttered the center, and straight-backed chairs were scattered everywhere. The long bar stretched along one side with small, square windows high up above it and narrow mirrors behind it. The mirrors were bedecked with small flags, a few guidons, and various bits of Indian regalia. Above them were mounted deer horns.

There were three men playing cards in the back, a few soldiers, and one bartender. Ki asked about rooms.

"We got a couple upstairs," the barman said. "How many of you is they?"

"Just two. A woman and myself."

"A woman? She ain't your wife?"

Ki smiled. "No. We happen to be traveling in the same

direction. How much for two rooms?"

"Fifty cents each for the night."

Ki put down the money, and the barman swept it into a box. "You go outside, round the side of the building, and you'll see the stairs. Stable's out back. If you wants feed you see the boy."

Ki asked, "Any strangers in town?"

"Jest you 'n' them soljers that I know of."

"Is there any law here?"

The bartender nodded. "We got a marshal, keeps the peace, sort of. They gits out of hand now 'n' then, tempers does. We don't got a jail. Marshal chains 'em to a post till they sobers up."

Ki nodded. "Thanks. Is there a place to eat?"

"Oh sure. Jillie's place is next door." The barman went to serve the troopers.

Ki went out to the short porch. "We've got rooms upstairs. There's a place to eat next door," he pointed, "and we're the only strangers in town."

"We may be looking in the wrong part of the world."

Ki shrugged. "Since we don't know, it's as good a place to look as any."

"Very philosophical." Jessie pulled her blanketroll off the horse and went up the steps.

Ki took the horses around to the stable. A young boy there was dozing on a cot. He sat up at the sound of the horses and stretched. Ki said, "You the stable man?"

The boy grinned. "Yeah."

Ki pulled off his blanketroll and both rifles. "We're staying upstairs for the night." He gave the boy a coin. "Feed 'em and rub 'em down, all right? What's your name?"

"Paco."

"Who runs this town, Paco?"

"Guess that'd be Charlie Roulette. He owns the Red Dog and the dance hall and the general store."

"You ever hear of a man called Preacher?"

Paco shook his head. "No . . . They was a preacher in

38

town here a year ago, but they called him something else . . ."

"Thanks. If you hear of him, let me know, all right?" He flipped the lad another coin.

Paco bit his lip. "Are you a Chinaman?"

"No. Half Japanese." He smiled and went out.

A scruffy-looking wagon drawn by two black mules came rolling into town very late. There were two men on the box, and the wagon looked empty, except for a tarpaulin fastened low over the bed.

There was no one awake to see it, no lights on anywhere. The wagon halted between buildings, then went on to the stream and stopped again with the mercantile store not far away.

Preacher looked round at the cottonwoods. "This ain't bad, you figger?"

Esek said, "I don't think we oughta camp here. Let's keep a-going."

"My butt's tired." Preacher got down stiffly. "They ain't no law here worth a damn, and we outa tobacco."

"All right. We git the tobacco, then go."

"In the morning. Store's closed now." Preacher sighed and looked at the shorter man. "If anybody asks, we'll say we's lost. Folks get lost all the goddam time."

"Yeah, all right." Esek studied the several dark buildings and frowned at the stream. Preacher was willing to take a lot more chances than he was, that was certain. He had argued for an hour about coming to Terrill. Sometimes Preacher was too damn sure of himself.

Esek said, "We ain't got any hard money. Nothin' but them baubles."

"We'll trade 'em something. They gets trade all the time. And they's plenty we needs besides tobacco."

"What you gonna trade?"

"How 'bout some of them gold rings?"

"You better hammer 'em flat first . . ."

Preacher looked pained. "Now wouldn't that look suspicious!"

"Then nobody could tell what they was."

"Who goes around with a lump of gold in his pocket? Jeez, Esek, you sure jumpy tonight."

Esek growled. "I d'want my damn neck stretched." He watched Preacher rummage in the back of the wagon, and frowned at the ring Preacher held up.

"This'n ain't got a mark on it, t'tell who owned it."

"Does it fit?"

Preacher tried the ring on. "It's loose . . ."

Esek reached for it. "It got a design on it. What the hell is it? Looks like a lizard."

"I think it's a dragon." Preacher put the ring on and turned it this way and that. "Yeah, it's a dragon." He put the ring in his pocket. "Let's get us some sleep."

They woke at sunup and boiled coffee. Preacher prepared to go into the store. "You want anything but tobacco?"

"Get some cheese."

Preacher nodded, put on his hat, and went around to the front of the store. The storekeeper was a big, expansive man with a red face and heavy arms. He wore a checkered shirt under a dirty apron and frowned at the ring Preacher took off his finger. He was used to barter, but not to gold rings. Most folks had simpler objects to trade. He took the ring out to the light, and when Preacher was looking the other way, he tried to bite it, but his tooth left no mark. Was it really gold?

"It's fourteen-carat gold," Preacher said gravely. "I paid a hunnerd dollars for it five year ago in St. Louie. Happen I was a big winner at the time."

"I'll hafta show it to Mr. Roulette. He owns this here store."

"Ummm. That goin' to take a lot of time?"

"I'll send a boy over to him with it. You camped somewhere near?"

"Out back by the stream. Names Brisco."

40

"Fine, Mr. Brisco. Sorry I got to do 'er this way . . ."

Preacher waved his hand and went to the door.

"I'll send the boy for you."

Preacher nodded and went back to the camp.

An hour passed, and a long-legged boy, who was wearing a shirt several sizes to small for him, came to the wagon. "Mr. Brisco here?"

Preacher got up and went back to the store with him.

The storekeeper said, "It's worth twenny dollars, Mr. Brisco, if you take it in trade."

"That all—twenny dollars!" Preacher pretended dismay.

"I sorry. Mr. Roulette said take it or leave it. I got nothing to say."

Preacher sighed as if deeply affected. He took an emotional pause, then sighed again. "Well, we got to have grub . . ."

★
Chapter 7

In the Red Dog Saloon, Ki idly watched a game of poker. The dark man with tight curly hair was Charlie Roulette, and he was showing off a ring he'd just bought, saying that when he got to St. Louis next, he'd have a diamond set into it.

"This here's a dragon," he said. "I'll have the diamond put right into his eye."

"It's a perty ring, all right," one of the cardplayers said.

"Where'd you get that ring, Charlie? Can I see it?" another asked.

Charlie held it up. "Took it in trade."

The cardplayer leaned in, looking at it closely. "It's got a animal carved on it . . . I seen that ring before!"

Roulette frowned. "What you mean?"

"It's got a dragon on it. That ring belongs to Tim Stoddard!"

Roulette placed a derringer on the table. "What're you sayin', friend?"

The cardplayer stared at the gun. "All's I'm saying is I seen that ring or one just like it. It belonged to Tim's pa, 'fore he died. He got it in China, he said." He swallowed. "It musta been one just like it."

"Yeah, one just like it." Roulette glowered at the other man. "Whyn't you take a walk, friend?"

The cardplayer began to get up, but two bartenders lifted him out of the chair, propelled him to the front door, and tossed him into the street.

Roulette said, "Whose deal is it?"

Ki went upstairs slowly. Jessie said, "What is it?"

"I just saw a ring." He told her what had been said. "What if that ring was part of the loot from an Indian raid?"

"Did Roulette say where he got the ring?"

"He said he took it in trade."

She gazed at him pensively. "Doesn't he own the general store?"

"Yes, he does," Ki said. "He could have gotten it that way. Somebody swapped it for groceries."

"Maybe our friend, Preacher."

Ki nodded. "The store's closed now. I'll go over there in the morning."

The next day, the storekeeper said, "Sure, I remember the ring. I sent it over to Charlie Roulette. He said to give twenny dollars in trade for it."

"Who was the man who had it?"

"What's the matter? You figger it was stole?"

Ki smiled. "I don't know. I only suspect I know something about the man who had it. Did he tell you his name?"

"Said it was Brisco."

Ki made a face. "That's not the name."

"Said he was camped over by the stream in back of the store. M'boy said they was two of them and a wagon."

"Your boy? He saw them too?"

"Yeah. He took the ring to Charlie."

"Can I talk to him . . . the boy, I mean?"

"Sure. He works over at the stable behind Rhomer's. His name's Paco."

Ki smiled again. "Oh. I know him. He took care of my horse. Thanks."

He went around the building and walked down by the stream. The wagon was gone, but there was a blackened fire circle. He knelt to feel the spot; it was still warm. Had Preacher and his companion been here?

Paco said, "The man was tall and lanky, kind of stooped, and dressed in black. The other one was shorter."

"Did they call each other by name?"

"I didn't hear no names . . . 'ceptin' Brisco."

"They had a wagon . . ."

"Yeah. It was kind of brown, dark brown. They had two black mules."

"Did you see anything in the wagon?"

Paco shook his head. "They didn't have no load. There was a sort of bundle, but nothing else except bedrolls."

"Thanks," Ki said. He gave the lad another coin and went upstairs.

He said to Jessie, "I think it was Preacher. We missed him by a few hours."

"No telling where they went?"

"No." He told her about Paco. "According to him, they had no load in the wagon, so they had probably just come from meeting the Indians."

"You're sure about the Indians?"

He shrugged. "No, but who else? Would it make sense for two gun smugglers to meet other whites on the prairie to do business?"

"It would not."

"Let's get back to Leavenworth. If they're getting guns, that's a big town . . ."

Running Wolf, acting on Preacher's information, sent four braves to watch the trails leading west from Leavenworth. And Preacher was proved exactly right. A wagon train appeared, escorted by horse soldiers, and took the trail west that led to Fort Carson.

One man rode back to inform Running Wolf; the others followed the wagons.

Sitting by a low fire, Running Wolf stared into the coals. A woman brought him slivers of meat on small, pointed sticks, and he ate them, hardly tasting the meat. The whites were changing things. Every wagon train that ventured onto the plains was escorted by troopers. One was like another. There had been a time when this was not so, but no longer.

He did not fear the troops, but it was prudent to respect their rifles. If he lost too many young men to army sharpshooters, his followers would grumble that Running Wolf's medicine was failing.

He knew the wagons in the train were loaded with supplies for the far forts—why else send them? To attack and loot the wagons it would be necessary to draw the troops away first. How could he do that?

He chewed the meat and thought back to the days of the missionary school. The white teachers had told them that in ancient times, far away across a great ocean, there had been wars and defeats. As a boy it had all seemed hazy and unreal; he could not envision a great ocean . . . except that it must be like the vast prairie. A prairie composed of water.

As a youth he had been very interested in the wars that had taken place far across this mysterious ocean. Was not he himself born to be a warrior?

And now he was one. And if he did not stop them, the whites would build cities and towns here, where his people hunted. The white-eyes did not live by hunting, and so they crowded together in towns and connected the towns with roads—and the roads brought more whites.

Were they never satisfied?

He feared the soldiers because of their rifles. Too many of his young warriors had only knives and bows. It was necessary to get close to use the bows effectively, and if the yellow-leg soldiers were well led, they could keep bowmen at a distance.

But if they were poorly led, they might walk into an ambush. Then, very close, the bows were better than guns, because they could shoot faster and they were silent.

Jessie and Ki rode by night, holed up during the day, and kept a careful watch for hostiles. But it was a vast, empty land, and they saw no other humans till they came close to Leavenworth.

45

Ki said, "If they're selling guns to the Indians, then we must go where people sell guns . . . and ask questions."

"We've already done that," Jessie said reasonably.

"How can we be sure they told us the truth? After all, we're strangers asking questions, not buyers to give the gun dealers profits."

"There's something in that," Jessie admitted.

There was no list of gun dealers in the town, so it was very difficult to find them. A few advertised in the newspapers, but it was necessary to go up and down the streets looking at signs. It was very slow work.

And after three days they had had no success at all.

Jessie did most of the questioning, using all her wiles to charm the dealers while Ki waited and looked for signs that the questioned was evading or playing loose with the truth.

After five days they were sure no one in Leavenworth had sold a man named Preacher a pocketknife.

Where were they getting guns?

"There are other towns," Jessie said.

Ki nodded. "Of course."

They bought a map of the area and began in the north and worked south, keeping the river on their left.

Returning to their house outside Leavenworth, Preacher and Esek went about their regular affairs, making sure certain people saw them, bartenders and the owners of harness stores where Esek did piece work.

Preacher delivered his fiery sermons wherever he could gather a crowd.

Esek too moved about, finding a day's work here and there, in livery stables and the shops of large companies that had extensive stables. He did not want to work exclusively for one firm, though he was offered jobs frequently.

And then he was taken on by the Patrick Iron Works for a day, and another day, and a third . . . They treated him very well and he was reluctant to leave.

The Iron Works had a large and busy yard on the riverfront. They manufactured iron stoves, firebacks, grave markers, pipe, fence parts, and hollowware, among other things. They also employed cutlers and wheelwrights and had twelve delivery wagons and a large stable of horses and mules.

Esek worked in the harness shop, which was next to the stable and only a step from the riverbank and the various wharves and piers along it. The Iron Works owned two big flat-bottomed barges, which were also used for hauling limestone and charcoal and occasionally for deliveries. Most of the firm's materials came from downriver on steamboats, which were busy as ants, puffing and whistling all along the Big Muddy, loading and discharging cargo on the docks.

During the first days of his employment there, Esek took note of the neighboring establishments. On one side was a cart and wagon manufacturer, on the other a row of warehouses with their lengths at right angles to the river. Crates, bales, and boxes were constantly being unloaded from steamers and either stored in the warehouses or hauled out the front and put onto delivery wagons.

It was while he was taking a morning breather with some of his fellow workers that Esek noticed the battered, dirty green stern-wheeler that came in and tied up at the pier of the nearest warehouse. A crew of near-naked, sweating negroes unloaded a number of long, obviously heavy crates.

The size and shape of the crates was very familiar. Esek strolled closer and leaned on the fence between the properties and was easily able to read the black-painted legend on several: 20 rifles Henry Cal .44 rimfire.

With a thumping heart he turned his back at once and lighted a short cigar. He had counted eighteen boxes! Twenty rifles to a box meant—360 rifles. Jesus! 360 rifles!

The Henry, he knew, was a 15-shot rifle, the forerunner of the Winchester. These were probably surplus arms and

47

had been sold to clear out an armory somewhere.

He puffed furiously. If he and Preacher could get their hands on those boxes, they could become rich!

That night, as he left the Iron Works, Esek walked his horse past the row of warehouses, looking hard at the first one, where the rifles were stored. On the front of each warehouse was the name Therry & Son. Each was a long, low building without windows, and each had a wide wagon door in the front, with a small Judas door inset, both heavily chained and padlocked. But the padlocks did not appear to be more formidable than others Esek and Preacher had forced. Esek did not see a watchman on duty.

As he rode home, he thought about New Orleans. Oh to be rich in New Orleans . . .

★

Chapter 8

When Esek got home, Preacher was heating the stew. He saw instantly that Esek was full of news. "What is it?"

Esek told him about the warehouse and the crated guns. "Three hundred and sixty rifles! If we sold them we could quit this business!"

Preacher nodded, his dark eyes lighting up. Guns for sale were scarce to begin with, and he and Esek could not buy many piecemeal without an enormous amount of trouble and lots of travel. If they pressed a dealer to buy too many, the man was sure to be suspicious—unless they had a very good story. Folks were reading about Indian raids in every newspaper.

"Draw a map of the warehouse and the river," Preacher said.

Esek flattened a scrap of paper and wetted a pencil. Laboriously he drew the Iron Works, the warehouses, and the river with its wharves. As he began to draw the road, Preacher stopped him.

"Not the road. We'll do'er from the river side." Preacher studied the drawing. "Find us a boat or a barge."

Esek brightened; he hadn't thought of breaking into the warehouse from the river. He'd been so concerned with the way wagon deliveries were made, he'd overlooked the possibility. That showed what a man could get conditioned to.

Preacher fiddled with the pencil. "We'll load them guns into a boat and drop down the river to a likely spot and transfer 'em to wagons." He tapped the map. "Them Henrys is good guns, all the same caliber too. Was there ammo with them?"

"I didn't see any. But I s'pose so."

"Well, it don't matter. The guns is the main thing." Preacher's brow furrowed. "Trouble is, we don't know if they's consigned to anybody—and they probably is. We'll have to snake 'em outa there fast as we can."

"I looked at the locks. We can bust 'em easy."

Preacher nodded. "They ain't a lock around can stand up to a good pry bar—or a hasp either."

"When d'you want to do it?"

"Soon's we can find us a boat. But there's one thing—"

"What?"

"You figger we'll need help?"

Esek thought about the husky crew he'd seen unloading the crates. But they had lifted them, two men to a box. He and Preacher ought to be able to do the same.

"I mean about the wagons."

Esek frowned. "The wagons?"

"Well, we can't be both places at the same time. Somebody got to meet us with the wagons, unless you figger we can leave them and the mules alone for the night."

"Oh . . . yeah." Esek put the cofffeepot on the stove. "Well, maybe we can . . ."

"I'd hate to hire somebody. It would sure as hell point a finger, huh?"

Esek nodded moodily. "It sure would." It would really mean taking a partner, and neither of them wanted that. They had done it at the Hitchens Armory, but no more.

On the other hand, how much of a chance would they be taking, leaving the wagons and mules alone for a few hours? Of course if some crook stumbled onto them, all he had to do was drive them away . . .

Preacher said, "I vote we take the chance."

"All right. And even if we lose the wagons, we still got the rifles and we'd be on the river."

"That's right."

Esek agreed. "Then let's take the chance. Whyn't you go riding down along the river tomorrow and look for a place."

Preacher nodded and poured out a cup of coffee. "We goin' to be rich, Esek. What you going to do with your money?"

Esek said promptly, "I goin' to New Orleans."

They spent two weeks talking to folks in small towns and turned up nothing. Jessie said, "Maybe they went out of business."

Ki shook his head. "Or they've gone somewhere else. We should have had a sniff before this."

They were in a hotel in Leavenworth having supper when Simon Strater came by and pulled out a chair. "How you all tonight?"

Jessie smile, "Fine, Simon."

"You both look tired."

"We've been trying to find someone," Ki said, "and we're not having any luck." Simon was a deputy sheriff who had given them help in the past.

"You want to find someone?"

"Two people, really," Jessie said. "Two men. The ones who robbed the Hitchens Armory and killed Colonel Dakins and a soldier."

"Ahhh. I remember reading about it. You have some leads?"

"We know a little," Ki admitted. "One's called Preacher. We have a sketchy description of them."

Strater nodded. "Why don't you go and talk to Cal Bates? Our office uses him sometimes to find people. He's got the nose for it."

Ki glanced at Jessie, who nodded. "Where is he located?"

Strater jotted down an address and passed it over. "Tell him I recommended him."

Cal Bates was a man about thirty, Jessie thought, tall and smiling. He lived in a small house on a tree-shaded street.

They found him in a workshop behind the house, where he was making furniture.

When Ki mentioned Simon Strater, he put his tools aside and took them into the house. He put the coffeepot on the stove and stirred the coals, laying on sticks.

"If Simon sent you, I smell trouble."

"We're looking for two men," Jessie said, and told him about the Hitchens Armory murders.

Ki said, "We're fairly sure they're selling guns to the Sioux, but they're elusive."

"One's called Preacher?" Cal rubbed his jaw. "It seems like I've heard something about a man like that . . ." He smiled at Jessie. "I have some informants. I'll spread the word." He poured coffee and handed the cups around. "If he's in Leavenworth we ought to hear something soon."

Preacher rode along the river in the morning and found several places where two wagons and teams could be hidden. He dismounted and tramped over the area; it was heavily forested and brushy. It seemed to him it would take a large slice of luck for someone from the town to stumble across them, especially in the dark. Why would anyone be walking along the riverbank at night anyway?

Satisfied, he went back into town and studied the riverfront. It extended for almost a mile, but only one central part was wharfed and kept dredged. There were half a dozen stern-wheelers tied up there and perhaps half a hundred barges, some empty and many piled high with goods under tarpaulins. There were also many small boats of all descriptions and sizes, some canoes, and even a few rafts.

Preacher sat his mount for half an hour watching the busy scene, then walked the horse slowly upstream, looking at the flat-bottomed craft. All were tied with ropes that could easily be cut. Along the bank, deeply embedded, were a dozen or more metal poles with iron baskets suspended from their tops. These were fire-blackened, some still smoking; they were used as torches. In the main area there were also ropes and wires with lanterns hanging from them.

Farther along there were no torches or lanterns. Preacher moved along this section very slowly, fixing it in his mind. It would be very dark at night.

A dozen or more small boats and canoes were tied there to several small piers that jutted out into the brown water; a few canoes were on the bank, upside down on wooden frames.

Preacher smiled and turned the horse toward home.

That night, when Esek came from the Iron Works, they discussed their plan and decided to make the attempt. It was the middle of the week, and the crated rifles might be hauled out and sent to their destination at any time.

Long after dark they drove their two wagons into town. Preacher led the way along the rutted road that paralleled the river. At the riverbank they halted, made a quick inspection to see that no one was about, then quickly loaded a canoe into one of the wagons. It was light and made no sound.

They drove two miles downriver on the winding road. Preacher had marked the turnoff with a small pile of stones, which he now kicked apart. He led the mules to the spot he'd selected and tied the teams. It was far from the road, in a small depression overshadowed by trees.

"Nobody'll see 'em," Preacher said confidently.

They slid the canoe into the water and paddled back upstream to the landing. Along the busy wharf area two steamers were loading, with lanterns flaring and gangs of men pacing back and forth with sacks and boxes.

Farther up, the waterfront was deserted and dark. Preacher had noted four or five flatboats, and when they approached the first, he hissed and they drew alongside it. It was about fifteen feet long and smelled of fish and oil, but was serviceable. There were half a dozen long poles in the bottom, and it was tied with a rope that Preacher easily cut.

Esek pulled the canoe out of the water, and they slipped aboard the flattie and pushed out into the stream. It took only a minute. They poled and sculled the flatboat upstream to the warehouse. The boat was pigheaded and obstinate, but they got the hang of it in half an hour and were able to outguess it and arrive at the warehouse dock in pitch darkness.

There were two broad steps up to the warehouse level from the riverbank, and a big lock on the door. Preacher took off his coat and held it wrapped tightly about the lock while Esek used a pry bar on it. There was a splintering rip as the hasp was torn out of the wood. It sounded loud in the still night. They waited a moment, but no outcry was raised.

"There ain't no watchman," Esek said.

Preacher pulled the door open wide and propped it. The cavernous warehouse was as silent and dark as the inside of a cave. Away from the door, Esek scratched a match and lighted the candle he'd brought with him. They stood in a small open space, and all around were boxes, sacks, and crates, piled to the ceiling, with tags bearing cryptic numbers.

It took five minutes to locate the rifle crates. They were neatly stacked near the front. "Maybe they was to be gone tomorrow," Preacher said. "Good thing we come tonight."

In the back, near a small, barred office, they found a four-wheeled cart. They lifted each crate onto the cart and trundled it to the back steps, then carried it to the flattie. It was slow, hard work, and it was three hours before all the crates were loaded onto the boat and their weight carefully distributed.

Esek closed the warehouse doors and wedged them shut. He and Preacher untied the flatboat and shoved out into the current. It was done.

"Three hunnerd and sixty guns, Esek," Preacher said in a low voice. "We's rich!"

★

Chapter 9

They continued their efforts to locate the elusive man who called himself Preacher. Ki visited saloon after saloon, asking questions. It was not proper for a woman to enter such an establishment, unless she was a person of ill repute, a soiled dove, so Jessie waited outside for him.

Unfortunately Ki found it necessary to order beer with each visit, because the bartenders as a class tended to ignore his questions if he did not buy.

Therefore, after half a dozen such visits, he was feeling very little pain, and Jessie took him back to the hotel to let him stretch out quietly.

This curtailed their activities.

Cal Bates came to the hotel in several days to talk to them. His informants, he said, had told him that a man called Preacher had indeed been delivering fire-and-brimstone sermons in saloons for some time . . . and passing the hat as a consequence.

Cal asked, "If he is giving sermons in saloons, why do you think he is running guns to the Indians?"

Ki said, "Can't he do both?"

Jessie replied, "Maybe he needs the money to buy guns."

Cal said, "How much money can he raise by passing the hat? He has to live too."

"What about the other one, the man he works with? Maybe he has money or a means of getting it," Jessie said.

Cal shrugged. "That's possible . . ."

Ki said, "You're forgetting—they robbed the armory. Doesn't that prove they're selling guns?"

Cal smiled. "Well, it probably means they sold *those* guns. Do you know of any others?"

Ki shook his head.

Jessie asked, "You said your informants said he *was* delivering sermons in saloons. Isn't he now?"

"No. No one's seen him for a while. Maybe they made a big score and are drinking it up. Those kind tend to spend it as soon as they get it."

Cal went downstairs with Jessie, while Ki remained in the room, stretched out. They had dinner together and he filled her in on his background. He'd been a newspaperman for a time, traveled to Europe and back, had owned several saloons, "But now I'm taking it easy for a while."

"And making furniture?"

He laughed. "That's just a hobby. Something to do with my hands."

"Simon told us you've been helping the local sheriff find people."

"Yes, because I know so many people involved in the saloon trade. I send the word out and pretty soon it comes back to me . . . Joe was seen here or there, or Tom did this or that last Saturday . . . that kind of thing."

"What do you really want to do?"

His answer surprised her. He said, "I want to run for Congress."

He smiled at her expression. "Don't you think I'd make a good congressman?"

Jessie laughed. "Of course. I'm sure you would . . . It's just—it's about the last thing I expected you to say. You're a man full of surprises."

"I hope so," he said, which surprised her again.

Moving downstream was easier. They only had to steer. Preacher took the tiller, saying he'd done it before. They let the river take them while they rested. Loading the crates had been the hardest work either of them had done since they were boys. They drifted past the lighted landing into darkness and nearly missed the place where the wagons and teams waited.

The flatboat was difficult to steer in slack water and was determined to yaw, but they finally got it poled against the soft mud of the bank and tied bow and stern.

Lifting the heavy crates out of the flattie and carrying them up to the wagons was harder than hauling them out of the warehouse. They cursed and strained, and it was nearly dawn before the task was accomplished.

"Jesus . . . ," Esek gasped, leaning against the wagon. "We dassen't go back through town—not tonight. They going to be one hell of a uproar when they find that warehouse door broke open."

"We'll go around," Preacher said. Esek was right. Some-one might remember the two men with loaded wagons on that particular night. No sense taking chances when every-thing had gone so smoothly.

Esek pushed the flatboat into the current and watched it glide away silently. It would probably nose into the bank somewhere, hopefully a long way downriver, and be found. Maybe the law would figure the thieves had gone downstream with the guns, rather than up.

Esek helped stretch canvas over the two loads, and then they headed into the prairie.

It was late in the afternoon before they reached their house and halted in the yard. But they were sure no one had seen them.

They hauled both wagons into the stable and left them with the guns in the beds. There was no other place to store them. Their hidden cache was much too small. It was a chance they had to take.

Esek rode off into town at midday, after some sleep, and told the foreman he'd been sick that morning but felt better now. He pretended great astonishment at the robbery that had taken place next door. The Iron Work employees were excited and chattering about it. And the police, Esek learned, were theorizing that a gang from across the river had done the looting, and a widespread search was being instituted.

Everything pointed to the probability that the guns had been taken downriver. Esek's fellow workers were of the opinion that the guns had been transferred to a steamboat and were probably well on their way to St. Louis. Esek agreed with them. "It's the only thing makes sense."

Preacher was delighted to hear that a gang was suspected. The nearness of the river had diverted everyone's thinking away from the land. It was an enormous bit of luck. Everything about the robbery had been lucky for them.

"Now all we got t'do," Preacher said, "is wait for word from Runnin' Wolf."

It was weeks in coming. One night there was a rapping on the back door, and when Esek opened it with a lantern and a pistol, three braves confronted him. One spoke passable English.

"Running Wolf send us."

Esek demanded, "Why'd he take so long?"

"Running Wolf hurt in battle wi' yellow-legs."

"Hurt! How bad?"

The brave shrugged bare shoulders. "He hit here." He touched his upper arm. "Bullet break bone."

"Damn," Preacher said. "How long'll he be laid up?"

The Indian looked puzzled.

Esek said, "How long he sick?"

The man shook his head. "Maybe one moon. He say I come again then." He turned to go.

"Wait," Preacher said. He motioned for two of the braves to stand by the door and led the other into the stable. He faced the man as he scratched a match and lighted a lantern. "Tell Running Wolf we have many guns. Very good guns."

"Many guns?"

"Hundreds. You know hundreds?"

"Hundreds?" The brave's eyes widened. He knew the word. His eyes changed then and he glanced around the stable. "Where you have guns?"

Preacher slapped the side of the wagon. "Right here." He unfastened the tarpaulin and pulled it back, disclosing the crates. With a pry bar he opened one crate and held up the lantern as the brave stared at the packed rifles. The brave said something under his breath.

Preacher slammed the box lid down. "Eighteen crates. You savvy eighteen?"

The man held up ten fingers, closed the hands, and held up eight more.

"That's right. Twenny rifles in each box."

The brave lifted the top of the crate and reached in to touch the rifles. He drew back an oily finger and gazed at it. Then quickly his face resumed its brown composure.

Preacher took him to the second wagon and showed him the crates. "More guns." He pointed to the painted legend on each box. "They enough rifles here to arm all your men."

The brave stared at the wagons.

"You tell Running Wolf what you seen?"

The man nodded.

He went back to his companions, and they mounted ponies without another word and were swallowed up by the night in moments.

Esek gazed after them. "D'you figger it's too many guns for 'em?"

"You mean will he be able to pay?"

Esek nodded. "That's what I mean. We're talking about thousands of dollars. That's a hell of a lot of money for an Indian. Maybe all the goddam tribes in the country ain't got that much."

Preacher frowned and bit the inside of his cheek. Had they been foolish? He hadn't thought it through. Esek was right. He said, "Maybe that was a big mistake . . . showin' him that many rifles."

"Yeah. And sure as hell Runnin' Wolf will want 'em all if I know him." Esek rubbed his chin nervously. He frowned at Preacher. "Now he knows we got 'em."

They stared at each other across the kitchen table.

Then Esek said, "He can't pay for that many. You figger he'll come and take 'em?"

Preacher grunted. He took down a bottle of whiskey. That was a thought that worried him exceedingly. He poured out two tumblers, half-full. In the past the Sioux had dealt with them because he had to—because he wanted guns. And they had treated him fairly—most times, except in the matter of whiskey—and the war leader had been fair with them.

But if Running Wolf couldn't pay for 360 guns, and he desperately needed them, wouldn't he do like Esek said— come and take them?

Preacher sipped the liquor. If he were Running Wolf and he knew where he could grab that many rifles, he damn well would come and take them. So why wouldn't the Sioux?

And not pay a goddam red cent for them!

Preacher made up his mind. "We got to hide them guns, Esek."

"That means we can't stay here then."

"Why not?"

Esek drained the glass. "Because if Runnin' Wolf comes here and doesn't find the guns, he'll make us tell him where they are. Indians are good at that, you know. He'll bake us over a slow fire till we tell him anything he wants."

Preacher gulped the rest of the whiskey. What Esek said was true! He hadn't thought that far along. But it was true, true, true. He sighed deeply, regretting what he'd done. "We shoulda showed him one'r two . . ."

"Too late now."

"Damn, Esek. Them guns're liable to be a millstone around our necks . . . with us goin' down for the third time. You got any ideas?"

"You don't think we could convince Runnin' Wolf we only got a few guns?"

"Hell no, not now. That damned Indian can count. He been to missionary school enough for that. He'll tell Runnin' Wolf we got three hunnerd and that's that."

Esek poured more whiskey into the glass. "Yeah. I s'pose so." He looked at Preacher. "Then we best move into town."

"Into town?"

"Yeah, get us a house there and shove them guns into it somewhere till we can figger what to do. That Sioux ain't comin' into town after us, that's for sure. Maybe we can sell the guns to somebody else."

Preacher nodded. Move into town! Yeah, they had to, didn't they? He said heavily, "All right, tomorrow I'll go get us a house."

★

Chapter 10

Cal Bates came to the hotel with news. There was a preacher holding forth over in Landsdale, about thirty miles north.

"He sounds like your man. You want to go look at him?"

"Certainly."

Ki saddled their horses and they went at once, an all-day trip on the winding road, with rifles across their knees against the possibility of an Indian sighting. The hostiles were known to raid to the very outskirts of a city. And they were getting bolder.

Cal entertained them with stories from his saloon days, and the time passed pleasantly. They saw no Indians, or other riders, and reached the town several hours after dark.

There was a hotel of sorts, and Jessie took a room and waited while Ki and Cal Bates made the rounds of the saloons, looking for the preacher.

They returned in an hour, saying the preacher hadn't shown up. Bartenders had told them the man hadn't been seen for at least a day.

Jessie had dinner with Cal, and she felt herself drawn to him. He was cheerful and self-deprecating and excellent company. And when her foot touched his under the table quite by accident, neither of them drew away.

In the evening they talked for a few moments with Ki, and then he went to make the rounds of the saloons. Cal said he should do the same, but instead he walked with Jessie to the end of town. And when they left the yellow flickering lights behind and stood under the vast carpet of glittering stars, he took her hand, curling his fingers around hers.

He said softly, "You're a beautiful woman, Jessica Starbuck."

"Thank you."

He faced her. "I'm not much with words . . ."

"Then don't say anything." She smiled and slid her arms about his neck, and he sighed, pulled her close, and kissed her.

Long minutes later he turned her about. "We came here to find out something . . ."

She laughed. "I think we found out."

He embraced and kissed her again.

In her hotel room she closed and bolted the door as Cal struck a match and lighted a tall candle. Then she was in his arms again, warm and yielding, their hungry lips meeting . . .

She drew him toward the bed, and he never quite knew how his clothes came off; her hands were everywhere, unfastening, helping—and they were suddenly naked, her arms encircling him, her velvety breasts caressing his panting mouth.

She captured his erect member and fondled it as they tumbled on the rumpled bed. He heard her delighted laugh, and his hands explored her firm thighs and rounded buttocks . . . And then all at once he felt himself entering her. They gasped and rolled on the bed; her knees came up high and she was on her back. He thrust and thrust again deeply and felt her arching her back and shuddering . . . The bed rocked under his wild pounding . . . and then . . . ecstasy . . .

She slept in his arms, their bodies still embracing and his eager staff arousing each time they moved. She moaned softly as she slept, pressing herself against the staff and writhing so that it came into her, her dreams coming and going throughout the night.

Ki sat in the Platte Saloon and listened to the man preach against various sins and errors and knew he was not the

63

person they sought. He was short and had a round belly and was clean shaven.

The man they wanted was tall and stooped and had a mustache—and was possibly a better speaker than this one. Ki slipped out before the hat was passed and went back to the hotel.

Jessie was not in her room. He sat downstairs and read a newspaper, then went to his room and to bed.

Preacher rode into town and asked around concerning a house to rent. A storekeeper said, "I thought you two was happy out there in the sticks."

"It's too far from town, and too easy for Injuns to sneak up on you. Besides, I got the Lord's work t'do and I can't spend all my damn time ridin' back and forth. I talk to that there horse's ears more'n I do to folks. You know where there's a house?"

"Well, the widow Jalder is thinking of sellin' out to go back to Chicago . . . she told me."

Preacher had no idea of buying, but he went to see her. She was in her eighties, tending her flowers in the yard and feeding birds.

"No, I got to sell, Preacher. Need the money to go back to Chicago."

"Peace, sister," he said.

Outside her yard he said under his breath, "You old bat!"

He stopped in two saloons and gabbed, asking questions, filching a few drinks, and quoting the Bible liberally. In the second a barman said he thought he recalled Nat Wilbur saying something about renting . . . maybe selling, he wasn't sure.

"Who's he?"

"Nat runs the bakery over a street or two. You go talk to him."

Preacher did. Nat Wilbur was a skinny type with bloodshot eyes and a hangdog look. Preacher said, "Peace, brother. I hear you all got a house."

"I might have. Damn good house too."

"Don't swear in front of me, brother. I'm a man of God. Where is this here house?"

"It's on Ninth Street, down thataway, about the edge of town." Nat pointed. "It's got a good roof, a stable, and a board fence. The privy was dug only two, three months ago. You could get another year out of it. There's a couple chinaberry trees and—"

It sounded exactly like what they wanted. "You livin' in it now?"

"Yep. Me and my woman."

"You lookin' to sell or rent?"

"Sell. We can live upstairs here."

Preacher went to see the house at midday, accompanied by the baker. The man was right. It was a good house, although it was full of junk and dirt. It would need one hell of a good swabbing out. The man's wife was probably the worst housekeeper west of Connecticut. It had two small bedchambers side by side, a parlor, a kitchen with an inside pump, a pretty good cookstove, and a fireplace in the parlor for heat. Off the kitchen was a wide back porch. The stable had two stalls and an alley door and was larger than the one they had. It also had a loft. Preacher smiled at that; they could shove the guns up there.

And it was only a spit and a holler from the open prairie.

"Like to rent it," Preacher said.

Nat shook his head. "Got to sell."

"If I rent it, you'll have money comin' in every month."

That was a good argument, but the baker overcame it. "Nope, got to sell."

His wife joined them and said the same thing. "Got to sell."

Preacher sighed, staring at Mrs. Wilbur. She was as skinny as her husband, and he wondered if their bones made much noise when he was atop her. It was not something he could discuss with them.

He asked, "How much you want?"

"We got to have three hunnerd dollars," Wilbur said in a defensive tone.

Preacher was astonished. "That's a hell of a lot of money, brother!"

"I thought you didn't swear."

"Forgive me." Preacher rolled his eyes skyward. "I was took by amazement. I hear so much cussin' from folks, it rubs off now'n then. But it's a lot of money!" He was thinking that if Wilbur throwed in the woman it might be a deal. She might have a little dash left in her . . . with the right man. Wilbur sure as hell wasn't the right man for anything, in Preacher's opinion.

Wilbur hemmed and hawed and finally came down to two hundred, but wouldn't budge from that. They finally hammered out an agreement after Preacher insisted they leave the carpets on the floors. He had taken a fancy to the red turkey carpet in the parlor.

They signed a paper, and Preacher paid over fifty dollars in hard money. They would make it all legal at the bank next day, when Preacher would cough up the remainder.

"How soon'll you all be out of the house?"

The woman said, "A week."

Preacher shook his head. "Out of the question, friends. I got to move in two days."

"That's impossible!"

"Then gimme my money back. It's no deal, brother."

Wilbur gave in reluctantly.

Esek was delighted and surprised when Preacher told him that evening. They had two hundred saved. Things were going their way!

"You said it's right on the prairie . . . ?"

"Yeah, only a minute away or so. And they's an alley behind the stable. But I been thinkin', Esek. It might be better if we didn't deal with them damn Indians. We got us a wad of them watches and rings and other crap and Runnin' Wolf is gonna give us more. We'd be runnin' a goddam pawnshop."

"Ummm." Esek nodded. "You got a better idea?"

"No. Not yet. What we got to eat? More stew?"

"There's some I can heat up."

"Yeah, good. I hungry as a coyote with a mouthful of feathers." He got up from the table and pushed sticks into the stove while Esek unwrapped a cloth from around a bowl of stew and set the bowl on the stovetop.

Preacher said pensively, "They's half a dozen fire-eatin' gangs roaming around. The papers is full of their doin's. Why can't we sell the guns to them?"

Esek made a face. "Yeah, but how we going to locate them? You s'pose they got any more than Runnin' Wolf?"

"They ought to . . ."

"I'll ask around. See what turns up."

A day later they moved what little furniture they had, piling it atop the crated guns to hide them. They hauled it all through town in the early afternoon.

Wilbur and his wife had moved out without lifting a broom. The rooms were dusty, the windows grimy with years of scum, and the walls streaked. With all the furniture out and the few pictures off the walls, the house looked miserable inside.

It took two days to swab it all, and in the meantime they slept in the stable. It was cleaner.

The guns were out of sight in the stable loft, partly covered with straw. No one would suspect. When they were finished and moved into the house, Preacher poured out two stiff drinks and they clinked glasses in the kitchen.

"Here's to the new house."

Esek said, "We's city folks now, with neighbors on each side. Got to watch our particulars." He cocked his head. "You figger we could sell that house out there in the sticks?"

"It wasn't ours. Anyhow, who would buy it?"

"Runnin' Wolf," Esek said, and they laughed.

★

Chapter 11

All their attempts at finding the man called Preacher, and his companion, had proved futile.

"We've been looking in the wrong places," Ki said. He spread a map out on the table in Jessie's hotel room. He drew a large circle around Leavenworth, embracing all the towns they'd visited.

"We have to go outside this circle."

Jessica frowned. "It's wilderness. The wild tribes own all the land there."

"Not all. There's towns." Ki pointed them out. "Some much bigger than Terrill. Indians don't raid towns. I suggest we start here." He circled a town name. "At Galesburg."

"That's a long way west . . ."

Ki made pencil marks. "We can go from Galesburg to Wister, to Norton, to Baileyville and back here. If we haven't learned anything, then we take the next loop."

"How will we get there?"

"We'll have to wait for army patrols to escort us, or go along with a wagon outfit, or both. We don't dare go alone."

When they told Cal Bates, he was against the idea. "It's much too dangerous!" When he was alone in her room with Jessie, he touched her hair. "I can't bear to think of this on a coup stick of some brave. Please don't go! I'll hold my breath the entire time you're away!"

She laughed, then kissed him tenderly. "I must. I've been in dangerous places before. And I have Ki to watch out for me."

"Can he do it?"

"Oh yes." She smiled. "Ki is indestructible. He *is* a weapon. Never fear, he'll bring us both back safely."

They stood by her bed, and a pale breath of light came from the half-open window. Her arms slid about his neck, and she lifted her chin to be kissed again.

Then somehow they were on the bed and her filmy gown had disappeared—how had she done that?

He drew in his breath, leaned down, and kissed her naked breasts, hearing her soft moans of delight.

She unfastened his belt buckle and he wriggled out of his jeans, pushing off his boots so they clunked on the floor. Then suddenly she was astride him and slowly letting herself down on his hard spike. She moved sensually as he caressed her and licked her nipples.

She bounced up and down on the rampant staff, driving him to near distraction. He thrust upward frantically, embraced her, and finally rolled her onto her side, still driving the spike into its lair. Her shapely legs held him in a death grip, and the bed groaned and protested as he plunged himself into her sinuous depths . . . and exploded . . .

They lay together with deep sighs and she felt a great contentment . . .

They left at dawn to ride to Galesburg, only some thirty miles away, a little longer by the road. They accompanied several families with wagons; there were five mounted men, heavily armed, riding with them, and the trip was uneventful.

Galesburg was a windy, spare collection of buildings on the high plains, and no one there had heard of a man who called himself Preacher.

The town had a minister of the Methodist faith who had a wife and four children and had been in residence for five years, acting as spiritual leader and postmaster. He was a short, dumpy man with thick spectacles and long sideburns.

The next day they rode to Wister with a freighting company's wagons and rider guards—six wagons and six riflemen who ranged out on the prairie looking for trouble but found none.

It was a long journey, taking five days. On the third day several of the riflemen skirmished with a few hard-riding Indians, but no one was hit and the redskins did not come close to the wagons.

Wister was a larger place than they had expected. It was also on the telegraph, though the wires were often cut. Indians cut them for the copper.

There were eleven saloons in the town, but no Preacher.

It had been a hard journey, and they stayed, resting up for several days, bathing, and sleeping in real beds.

Then Ki came in with news. "There's a wagon train making up for Norton, and they're going on through Baileyville to Leavenworth! I think we can join them."

"I'll get my things together. When are they leaving?"

"Probably in the morning. I'm going to see the wagon master now. You agree?"

"Yes, of course. There's nothing here for us."

He nodded and went out.

The wagon master's name was Monk Tregar. He was a big, rough-looking man with black hair and mustache. He greeted Ki pleasantly and seemed glad of another two rifles—till he heard one of them was a woman.

"I don't know about that, Mr. Ki."

"Call me Ki. The woman can shoot as well as anyone and she's afraid of nothing." He smiled. "And she'll brighten up your train."

When Monk saw her, he withdrew his objections. She *did* brighten up the train. She wore jeans and a checked shirt, and her blond hair was gathered in the back with a black ribbon. She came riding in with Ki, a Winchester across her rounded thighs and a Colt on her hip, and men stared and forgot to breathe.

Monk said, under his breath, "Jesus Christ! I don't believe it!"

But she was real. She smiled at all of them as Monk scattered the men, yelling at them to get about their jobs.

At the last minute a troop of cavalry clattered up to the staging area, and the young lieutenant introduced himself. "I'm Lieutenant Sims, sir. I'm going along with you to Norton."

"Glad to have you, Lieutenant. How many you got?"

"Thirty men, sir. We're heading for Fort Perry. We'll leave you somewhere east of Norton in fact."

"Good."

Ki talked for a bit with Monk, telling him they were looking for two men. "Maybe you've seen them . . . One's called Preacher, a tall, stooped man . . ."

"No, I haven't. You think they're somewhere out here?"

"They have to be somewhere, yes."

"This here prairie is a sea of grass stretchin' from the Shining Mountains a thousand miles east. You know what you're up agin?"

"Yes, but we have to look . . ."

It was still dark when Ki rolled out and called to Jessie. The wagon train was stirring. A dozen lanterns had been strung along the roadway for light as men and animals stomped and milled, the men swearing at the obstinate mules, who seemed determined not to be pushed into harness and shafts.

Monk and his assistants were everywhere, growling and helping. And at last they were ready . . . and Monk shouted, "S-t-r-e-t-c-h out . . ."

There was little danger from hostiles in the first miles. The cavalry rode ahead, and they took the dusty trail, settling down, facing the stiff breeze that came from the west.

The second day out they came to a tiny settlement that had no name, but it had a saloon. It catered to travelers, the bartender-owner said. "Mostly wagon men. They comes through here regular. You bring any news?"

Monk told him what he knew and Ki asked about Preacher. The man had not been seen here.

One of the wagon men came in and asked about girls.

The owner said, "They's four girls upstairs, friend."

"Respectable women?" Monk asked.

The owner looked astonished. "What in hell would anyone in a place like this want with a respectable woman?"

The wagon train pulled out as soon after dawn as it could. Monk had a half dozen men move ahead. "Take a look-see out on the grass. You might scare up something, but stay together."

Ki said, "You think Running Wolf might be watching us?"

"No way to know. But if I was Runnin' Wolf and interested in what was in the wagons, I'd be watching."

"It must be cold, sitting out there . . ."

"I hope it freezes his ass."

Lieutenant Sims had his men deployed in the rear. It was a place of much danger. Indians were fond of hitting where they weren't expected.

But the day passed from morning to noon and afternoon, and all was peaceful. "We're well protected," Ki said to Jessie. "A patrol in front and soldiers behind. Plenty of warning if the Sioux have ideas of attacking."

She said, "I heard men talking about some place called Beaver Wash. They seemed to think it was especially bad medicine—for us."

"Oh? I'll ask Monk."

And when he asked, Monk scowled. "It's a sandy wash, half a mile wide, or more. We'll come to it tomorrow. Probably no water in it . . ."

"What worries you?"

"Ambush. It's the best spot for an ambush along the entire trail . . . maybe in the entire territory."

Monk was worried, right enough. It was very apparent. Wagons might get stuck in the sand, or get spread out

72

because some were faster than others. It would be a miserable place to get hit by the hard-riding Sioux.

And of course the Sioux knew it.

They had about twenty men, counting drivers, who could handle rifles, and the thirty troopers—would they be enough?

Ki said to Jessie, "Maybe the Sioux are nowhere near here. They can't be everywhere."

"With rifles bought from Preacher and his friend."

"Yes. That crossed my mind too."

★

Chapter 12

The hue and cry raised after the warehouse robbery lasted for more than a week. But the police had few clues to work with. The theory that the crates had been taken either across the river or downstream seemed the most likely, and apparently no one thought to look closer to home.

A reward of five hundred dollars was offered for information leading to the recovery of the guns, then the matter seemed forgotten.

Preacher made his rounds of the saloons, cadging drinks and giving advice—not sermonizing as he once did. It took too much time to give sermons. He soaked up information about several of the more active political factions.

The most talked about was led by a man known as Big Bill Yellen. Bill hung out at the Roden Theater and Saloon, often holding what he called political meetings in the theater when it was closed to the public. Tim Roden, the owner, was one of Bill's followers.

Bill Yellen proved to be easy to find, and Preacher actually went so far as to buy him a drink—which was against everything he stood for. Others bought *him* drinks.

He introduced himself as Preacher Chaney Hanks. "I heard fine things about you, Mr. Yellen. Thought I'd look you up."

"Call me Bill, Preacher. What you want?"

Preacher saw a big, burly man with a black beard and shining eyes that were hard as agates. Bill's hands were twice the size of an ordinary man's, and his huge shoulders strained the coat he wore. But the coat was old and stained, and his boots were scuffed and run over. Bill did not look prosperous. Did he have the money to buy guns?

"Folks say you want to change the laws. That so?"

"Damn right. Laws is agin the right folks. You for me or agin me?"

"I'm for you, brother. I'm agin them fools in Washington City. I hear you got two hunnerd men at your back."

"Hell, I got more'n that," Bill said, thinking that maybe this preacher could be an asset. A man of God could be a big help showing the right way to the hayseeds pushing on plow handles.

Preacher asked, "Is all them men armed?"

Bill was surprised at the question. "Well, sure, one way or the other. What good's a man without a gun?"

"Just askin', brother."

"It ain't no secret, Preacher. Things is shapin' for a showdown."

Preacher glanced around the saloon. No one was close, but he lowered his voice. "You all in the market to buy some guns, Bill?"

Bill became wary all at once. His eyes widened as he stared at the other man. "You a preacher and you sellin' guns?"

Preacher nodded. "The Lord has marched into battle afore now, brother."

"What kind of guns?"

"Rifles. Fifteen-shot rifles."

"How come a preacher doin' this?"

"Preachin' is my trade, Bill. Happen I know where there's good guns to be had. Folks tells me things." He winked. His black eyes danced about the room and came back. "If you can't buy these here weapons, I'd take it kindly that you don't say nothing about 'em."

Bill grunted. "Folks tells you things, huh?"

"They do. And I'm tellin' you—you standing for what you do."

"What you want for the guns?"

"These ain't my guns, Bill. I'm talkin' for somebody else. But I seen 'em and they's good, damn good, not no junk. I swear it." Preacher lifted his hand as if taking an oath.

"How much?"

"Twenny dollars each. Hard money. And it ain't f'me."

Bill whistled. "That's a stiff price. How many you got?"

Preacher shrugged. "Maybe thirty or so. I ain't positively sure."

"Ummm. Where are they?"

"I dunno. But I think they might be across the river."

Bill thought about it. He needed rifles bad. Most of his men had punkin slingers and shotguns, guns they used around the farm. But of course everybody had those. Fifteen-shot rifles sounded good! And good rifles could make a difference.

But twenty dollars times thirty was six hundred dollars—cash!

He sighed inwardly. He and his group simply did not have that kind of money. Could he get it? He might. There were banks that might be drawn upon as political expediencies, six-gun withdrawals . . .

He said, "You dealin' with anybody else about this here commodity?"

"Not now."

"We talkin' cartridge guns . . ."

"Yeah. Henry rifles."

"Henrys! Where they come from?"

"I dunno. It wasn't my place t'ask. You unnerstand."

Bill nodded. "Let me talk to my bunch. It'll take a while to get the money. Where'll you be?"

Preacher waved his hand vaguely. "I be around. I never know where I go tomorra. But I come back here to the theater ever' few days. How's that?"

"All right. And you keep shut about the guns."

Preacher smiled. "I'll do 'er. Peace, brother."

Esek was skeptical. "He didn't have the money right off but he's innerested? It might take a month to get it."

"All I did was talk to him," Preacher said irritably.

"And then if he takes twenny guns, we still got three hunnered."

"But dammit! We got the money!"

"Yeah, that's so . . ."

Preacher grumbled. "Sometimes I wish we never stole them damn guns. Sellin' them a few at a time is liable to get us tangled with the law."

Esek was silent. As usual Preacher got himself on both sides of an argument at the same time. It would probably not be politic to point it out. Esek got up, poured water into the pot, and set it on the stove.

Preacher said, "Maybe we ought to go out and find Runnin' Wolf . . ."

Esek shook his head. "He'd want 'em all, and pay us with junk."

"Well, what you think?"

Esek faced him. "We got to get shut of them rifles as quick as we can. You told Bill Yellen twenny dollars apiece?"

Preacher nodded. "But if we give 'em away he'll know they was stole, won't he?"

"That won't make a damn to him. You figger we can trust him?"

"Hell no. I'd trust Runnin' Wolf faster." Preacher sighed. "It's a pain in the ass us having to deal with crooks the way we do."

Esek grinned and shoved wood into the stove. He put coffee into the pot and stirred it. He agreed that probably the Indian was more honest than Bill Yellen. Running Wolf wasn't as sophisticated and didn't have the advantage of civilizing thoughts and forces.

Preacher said, "What about Runnin' Wolf? He knows we got the guns."

"And forget about Bill Yellen?"

"We ain't married to him."

Esek frowned. "What if he comes lookin' for us?"

"By then we'll have something from Runnin' Wolf. We'll pack it up and take a steamer. To hell with Bill Yellen."

"Just the other day we was talking about not being in the pawnbroker business. We got a hunnered watches now from that damn Injun. You want more?"

Preacher growled. "I want t'get shut of these guns same as you do. Runnin' Wolf seems like our best bet. Even if we do have to take his junk. There's good articles with it. We can sell them watches and rings. I got twenny dollars in trade for one of 'em out in the sticks, didn't I?"

Esek nodded. Getting rid of the jewelry would take time, that was all. Maybe they could sell the entire shebang somewhere like New Orleans.

He said, "How'll we find Runnin' Wolf?"

"We'll go to Bear Rock and make a smoke. One of his braves will come looking."

"And we'll take one rifle. Just one."

Preacher shrugged. "All right. That means we got to leave the guns sittin' there in the stable . . ."

"Nobody's going to be nosing around our stable, is they? Besides, we'll only be gone a day'r two." Esek took the pot off the stove. "Hold out your cup." He filled Preacher's mug. "Does Bill Yellen know where we live?"

"I didn't tell 'im."

"When you want to go to Bear Rock?"

★

Chapter 13

They reached Beaver Wash in the middle of the morning. Jessie looked at it critically. The yellow-gray ground was half a mile across, or a little more, a tortured route of rock, sand, muddy brown rivulets, and a deeper sparkling flow.

Were the Sioux watching them from the far side? Everyone in the train was thinking ambush, Jessie knew. She saw Monk and several others studying the area.

Ki said, "Are the Sioux there?"

"Why not go up or down, go around them?"

He shook his head. "No difference. If they're over across there, they'd only follow."

"Then what's Monk going to do?"

"I think he'll push across with riflemen in the first wagons. Without the problem of the Indians, the wash would be no hazard. But from their point of view, the wash is ideal. The Sioux are in cover and we're out in the open."

Ki used his binoculars on the far side. He said to Monk, "I think I just saw a glint of something, Monk. Like sunlight on a rifle barrel." He passed the glasses over.

Monk focused them. "I expect they're there all right." He handed the binocs back.

There was no telling how many Indians faced them, Ki knew. Now they were invisible, but when they charged, it would be in a rush, suddenly, with hideous yells and yips and a thunderous clatter of hoofs. The Indian's best weapon was surprise—and he knew how to use it. The sudden charge was calculated to throw an enemy into a panic, to make him lose his head at the very moment he should have all his wits about him. It was a weapon that had worked too well, too many times. Ki hoped it would not work today. Of course Monk, as wagon master, would do his best to see that everyone was prepared and loaded for bear.

The wagons were halted at the edge of the wash, and Monk prowled up and down the line on his horse, restless, like a mother hen with a gaggle of chicks.

He said to Ki, "There's one damn thing I can't do nothing about."

"What's that?"

"The mules. If them Injuns kill the mules, we're done for. They'll have our hair."

"They can't kill them all!"

"They'll try . . ."

"Not if we can keep them at a distance. We've got plenty of good shots."

"Yeah . . . I'll tell 'em to shoot at anything that moves." He turned his horse.

Lieutenant Sims and his thirty troopers halted at the edge of the wash. Sims rode out a few yards and used his glasses, searching the opposite bank.

Ki studied the far side with his binocs. A thousand men could easily be hidden there, motionless as stones. And no one could lie as motionless as a Sioux. He gave the glasses to Jessie.

Sims came back and said to him, "You think they're there?"

"A Sioux can hide in his own shadow, Lieutenant. And when you get close enough he's deadly with his arrows." He did not think the youngster was impressed.

Then suddenly one of the troopers spoke excitedly, "Lieutenant! There's someone over there!"

Ki swung around and Sims leveled the glass again. "It's a—there's two of them! They're whites—running this way!"

Ki stood in the stirrups, shading his eyes. Jessie said, "They're small—"

Sims spurred forward, yelling. "Sergeant, those are whites! Take ten men and go get them!"

"Wait!" Ki shouted. "It's a trick!" He could see the figures. They were running hard and seemed to be children—but, no one was pursuing! He yelled, "Don't send men out there, Sims!"

The officer paid no attention. He spurred a hundred yards into the sandy wash. The sergeant collected the men quickly and dashed across the rutted ground toward the distant figures. Sims ordered the rest of the men forward, motioning them to spread out in a line.

Jessie and Ki watched helplessly. The man was a fool! It was an obvious trap. Ki glanced around, hearing Monk swear. "What the hell they doing?"

Ki dismounted and pulled Jessie down and behind the cover of a wagon. He saw the two running figures stumbling through the sand. One was dressed in boy's clothes, the other as a girl. They ran toward the soldiers—then suddenly fell flat.

Ki ducked, pulling Jessie down, and a fusillade of shots poured out. Powder smoke eddied and troopers' saddles were emptied. The shots continued as the troopers milled about in confusion. Riderless horses galloped along the wash, and a dozen bullets rapped against the wagons and cracked overhead. Out of the smoke troopers galloped away from the melee . . . five . . . six . . . ten, each bending low over his horse's mane.

Fourteen men returned. Sims was not one of them.

A sergeant called them together, dismounted them, and began attending to wounds. Out of thirty men, there were now twenty-one left. Nearly every man who had gone into the wash had been hit, some only superficially. They all looked shocked, Ki thought. Every man was pale and some were visibly shaking. None had expected to ride into a withering fire; every man had lost friends.

81

Across the wash, no longer in hiding, the Sioux were gathering in plain sight. They yelled and gestured, moving about on horseback. Ki tried to count them—more than a hundred, probably several of them hurt. A few fired off rifles as they celebrated their victory. He wondered if Running Wolf was their war leader.

Monk growled, "They weren't whites at all. They were Indians dressed in captured clothes. How long had Sims been out here?"

"Only about a month, sir. But the rest of us was fooled too." He had a long gash on his forearm, and the shirtsleeve was torn off.

Monk said, "I don't figger them to charge us. They'd lose too many. They'll yell and bluff—then they'll go home."

Jessie said, "Will we go across?"

"That's up to Monk. He's the boss here."

Perhaps fifty Indians had ridden to the center of the wash, brandishing spears and coup sticks, raising dust, but letting off steam. They probably had no intention of charging into waiting riflemen.

Jessie felt a terrible letdown at the loss of so many of the troopers, so suddenly. She had known none of them, but it was a tragedy. The young lieutenant had acted impulsively, foolishly—but it was done.

Glancing around, she saw that Monk was there, a rifle across his thighs, shaking his head. "I seen 'em pull that trick before. That dumb lieutenant should've asked us." He shaded his eyes. "How many's over there?"

"At least a hundred," Ki said.

"Yeah. Every time he wins, he gits more to join him. Pretty soon he'll have a regiment." He looked at the sun. "We ought t'get across that wash today." He let his breath out. "But maybe we ought to camp here and let 'em get it outa their systems. They all hotted up."

"I'd vote to try it tomorrow," Ki said.

"I think you're right." Monk had the wagons circled on the bank and had the horses and mules driven inside.

With the wagons up close, no Indian could ride his horse between them. Then he worked out a guard schedule with the sergeant.

It was a long night. Ki slept fitfully and woke many times, listening, but there was no alarm. The guards were alert and silent. But across the wash the Sioux kept up a constant yammering, yipping, and singing. Now and then one fired a rifle.

They were celebrating . . . and they had soldier scalps. Along with nine rifles and pistols, Ki thought. Weapons that would probably be used against them in the morning.

The sounds from the Indian camp died out several hours before dawn, and the prairie fell silent except for the night birds high in the dark.

With first light came several scattering shots that tore holes in canvas tops or hit wagon sides. They did no damage, but they were annoying. Sharpshooters fired back when they thought they had targets. It was impossible to tell if they hit anything.

To the wagon men Monk said, "We'll cross in pairs and I want you t'shoot at any damn thing that moves. I want every jasper with an itchy finger up front. When you see powder smoke from them Sioux rifles, I want six bullets on the spot in the next second. You hear me?"

The sergeant asked, "Where you want us, Monk?"

"Out to the sides. Make sure they don't hit us from there." He glanced around. "We'll move soon's we're ready."

It took a while for the first wagons to be placed as Monk wanted them, with the small horse herd in between. He put six men in each front wagon; each man with a rifle and two pistols.

He had the canvas tops removed for better visibility, and all the women, except Jessie, were sent to the rear wagons with the few children.

A few buzzards soared high in the still air as if expecting a battle to take place.

"All right," Monk said softly. "Let's go."

The first two wagons had clattered nearly a third of the way across the wash, closely followed by the others, when a fusillade of shots downed five mules. The wagons halted in their tracks, and instantly the riflemen replied with a furious fire, but the damage was done.

Monk swore, ducking as sniping shots cracked near him. Ki yelled at the others to fire at the muzzle flashes. The Indians were hard to see; they lay in sandy ruts, loading and firing, a hundred yards away. Jessie lay in one of the third-rank wagons and fired at flashes, several times seeing a hand or a leg thrown up, signs of a hit.

Wagon men ran forward at Monk's direction, cut the harness, and backed the lead wagons so that new teams could be hitched. The riflemen piled out and spread along the ground, crawling forward, firing, and crawling again.

At once the Sioux fire diminished. The Indians, unused to firearms, could not load as quickly or fire as accurately as men who had grown up with rifles. The steady advance continued as the Indians withdrew.

Then suddenly they were gone.

Ki and Monk mounted with half a dozen men and galloped forward, pistols in each hand, but the enemy had vanished. They found a litter of food, bones, and bits of clothing and equipment. Scattered about were half a dozen dead animals, torn uniforms, and half a hundred blackened areas where campfires had burned.

The bodies of soldiers, mutilated and torn, were found in the brush, hardly recognizable as human forms.

And there was a terrible stink in the air that nearly turned their stomachs.

On the far side of the wash, Monk halted the wagon train, and they dug a deep trench and buried the bodies. The sergeant sent his men into the wash to bring back stones, and a huge cairn was erected over the spot.

★

Chapter 14

Esek saddled two horses, and they left the town at midnight, walking the horses out to the prairie in the dark, meeting no one. After moving in, they had exchanged greetings with their neighbors, explaining that they might be away for days at a time on business. It was not the best situation, since neighbors were often close, but there was no help for it.

They rode steadily through the rest of the night and halted at sunup. They ate a cold breakfast, and Preacher groused with every bite. Running Wolf was wounded, he said, they had no idea how bad, and they might never meet with him. Some other war chief, not so easy to deal with, might now be in command.

Esek said, "Wait and see. Maybe it ain't that bad."

"I got a feelin' we doing the wrong thing."

Esek rolled his eyes. Preacher's moods were impossible! He wanted to tell the other man to keep his worries to himself, but he knew he might as well tell the sun to stand still.

However, they saw no one during the long ride and arrived at Bear Rock at dusk. They made a fire in the shelter of a half-cave, where a hundred fires had been made in the past, and boiled coffee and heated meat and beans.

Preacher had brought along a bottle, and several jolts from it helped to diminish his dark mood. With the guns safely in the stable at home, and the Sioux unable to come into the town—and not knowing where they lived—he felt more secure.

"But he knows we got em," Esek said. "And he'll have every damned one of 'em or we dassen't come out here again. If we do, we'll leave our hair."

"But that damned redstick ain't got it all his way. We can deliver a few at a time."

Esek agreed, but he did not believe it.

They made a good smoke in the morning when the air was still. It streamed up into the blue as Esek made a bonfire then piled on green wood. They kept it going for an hour.

In the middle of the afternoon five braves showed up, led by the same man who had come to their out-of-town house.

Without dismounting, he motioned to them. "You come."

"Where's Runnin' Wolf?"

"You come."

"Is he hurt bad?"

The brave shook his head shortly. He waited as they gathered up their utensils, rolled blankets, and tied them on. Then he led at a steady pace, north and west, never slackening.

They reached Running Wolf's camp long after dark. It was in a small valley where a stream meandered. There was a collection of tepees and a dozen small fires and very few women. They saw no children at all. Neither did they see Running Wolf.

The Indians left them standing, gave them nothing, and put out all the fires. Esek and Preacher rolled up under the trees and were awake at first light. They made a fire, ate what they had brought, and waited.

In an hour they were taken to see Running Wolf. He was in a tepee, lying on a buffalo robe, looking pale. His left arm was bound with a soft leather wrapping, but he was obviously recovering from the wound. They sat opposite him, and he regarded them expressionlessly from under thick black brows.

"You have many guns." It was not a question.

86

Preacher nodded. "Yes."

Esek had brought along one Henry rifle, and now he laid it in front of Running Wolf. "They just like this one. All the same caliber."

Running Wolf picked up the rifle with his right hand and looked at it carefully. He said something to the brave behind him, and a rattle of words were exchanged.

The brave took the rifle, cocked it several times, worked the lever, and listened to the action, then spoke again to Running Wolf and laid the rifle in front of him.

"I want guns," Running Wolf said.

Preacher nodded again. "You want guns . . . we want pay." He thought a steely light came and went in the other man's eyes, but the Sioux's tone did not change.

"I pay."

He said something to the brave, who immediately ducked out of the tepee and returned in a few moments with a heavy parcel. He dumped it in front of Running Wolf and stepped away. The war leader flicked the parcel open, and the two whites gazed at a gray canvas sack stamped with black letters: US Govt.

"Gold," Running Wolf said. He motioned to them, and Preacher opened the canvas flap and looked inside. There were rolls of dark paper with the ends tucked in. His heart beating rapidly, he reached in and brought out one of the rolls.

"Is that money?" Esek asked.

Preacher broke the paper, and gold coins suddenly flowed over his hand to the ground. "Jesus! Double eagles!"

Reverently Esek picked up a handful. Twenty-dollar gold pieces! They looked freshly minted. He had several hundred dollars in his hand, and the canvas pouch was full of them!

"Plenty gold," Running Wolf said. "You bring guns."

Preacher smiled. "We bring guns."

When they were alone, Preacher said, "They must be a dozen rolls in that sack. Them damn Sioux has raided an army paymaster."

"Or they broke into a gover'ment safe."

"And he never said a word till now—givin' us that jewelry junk! The son of a bitch."

Esek said, "How much is in that pouch, you figger?"

"Six, seven thousand easy. I didn't get to count all the rolls. If they all double eagles . . ."

Esek made a face. "Never mind. We didn't figger to get full price for every one. This here's a windfall."

Preacher lighted the stump of a cigar and grunted. They were huddled by a small fire, blankets pulled around them. They had told Running Wolf that in the morning they'd hightail it back to town to bring out the rifles. "You figger he's planning anything?"

"Runnin' Wolf? Hell, nobody can tell what's in that black skull of his. You think he got something up his sleeve?"

"Yeah. I think he didn't like it much that we only brought him one gun." Preacher glanced over his shoulder. "He didn't say nothing about us moving into town. Wonder if he knows it."

"It don't matter if he does." Esek laid more sticks on the fire. "It's that delivery that worries me."

"He might not pay?"

"He's a Injun, ain't he? Do Injuns got any honor?"

"Ummm." Preacher was silent a moment. "We'll have to promise him more guns then. We'll say this delivery ain't the last one."

"Yeah . . ."

Preacher smiled. "I wonder if he got any more gold?"

Jessie and Ki took rooms in the Baileyville Hotel, a ramshackle building next to the Alamo Saloon, and slept round the clock. The wagon train went on without them, into Leavenworth.

The next day Ki visited the seven saloons in town, but there was no sign of a man called Preacher. One bartender said such a man had been there several months ago . . .

Cal Bates called on them at the hotel, and listened to their tales of Indian fighting with worry lines in his forehead. A beautiful young woman should not be out fighting the Sioux!

Jessie said there were certain things that had to be done and could not be left to others. She asked, "Have you heard any word of Preacher?"

"No. He hasn't been seen in any of the saloons—at least not delivering his sermons. He could go in and out and no one would notice, I'm sure, unless he started preaching."

Cal rode back to Leavenworth with them and a half dozen wagons carrying buffalo bones picked up on the prairie. They saw no hostiles.

Preacher was cadging drinks in the Indiana Saloon when one of the bartenders leaned over the bar and spoke to him earnestly. "People been askin' about you, Preacher."

"What? What for? Was it the law?"

"I dunno who, but somebody askin'. They been here two, three times. Different people."

He managed a smile. "I ain't broke no laws."

"It ain't the law, Preacher. Somebody else."

Preacher nodded. "Thanks." It was probably someone from Big Bill Yellen. Bill wanted the guns and Bill didn't know where to find him. Preacher hadn't gone back to the theater as he'd said he would.

That night he told Esek, and Esek said a very sensible thing. "Stay outa saloons, Preacher."

Big Bill Yellen sent four of his followers to Hilgard, a small town east along the Missouri. Their object: to rob the local bank. He did not go himself, being too easy to recognize; no one would forget his bulk. Hilgard was a trading town, and though it had only one bank, it was a busy place.

Before the men went, Bill studied the plan with Virgil Cloud as they sat in the back of the empty Roden Theater. Virgil was a lanky, dark man with half an ear missing . . .

lost in a prison fight. He and Bill had been together in one scrape or another for a decade. Sticking up a bank was not a new experience.

Bill fiddled with a pencil. "The best way is to take a flattie down to Hilgard with the horses, so you don't meet nobody on the roads. You seen that bank before?"

"Yeah. Two, three times. It's right in the center of town, though."

"Hell, the town's not that big. It'll take you a minute to ride out. Lookee, here's what I figger." Bill drew a crude map of the area. "Hilgard's right here, on the river. You land the flatboat maybe three miles upstream. How many men you want to take, three?"

Virgil nodded. "Me'n three more."

"All right. Then you bring eight horses and—"

"Eight horses!? What the hell we need with eight horses?"

"Keep your shirt on. Eight horses and four saddles. You leave four of them horses right here." Bill-made an X on the map. "That's about ten mile from town . . . or a little closer if you see a good spot to hide 'em."

Virgil frowned. "That's miles south of the river."

"Yeah. You can't go back by the river. It'd be too slow. You got to make a big swing. When you leave the bank you go straight to the horses you got hid. Go as fast as you can, especially if there's a posse behind you. Make 'em chase you hard as hell."

Comprehension dawned in Virgil's face. "Then we'll have fresh horses!"

"That's right. While them farmers is coming after you on tired out nags. You make a swing like I said and come in here in three, four days. Come in easy at night."

Virgil bared his teeth in a big grin. "And they ain't a telegraph in that whole damn country. That's a real good plan, Bill."

"We need a thousand for the guns. Don't come back with less."

"We'll get all we can." Virgil found a cigar and looked at it critically. "You going to *pay* for them guns, Bill?"

"I got to pretend." Bill smiled. "Preacher, he wants to count the money. We'll let him count it, but that don't mean he puts it in his pocket. He'll count it and tell us where the guns are."

Virgil nodded, lighting the cigar. That was a good plan too. The guns *and* the money.

He stole a flatboat at night and took it downstream a mile or so, to where the others were waiting with the horses. He had picked Eli Grove, Jud Walsh, and Dewey Sohl. Eli and Jud were cousins who had worked together many times. They were wanted in Oklahoma and Texas for several items. Dewey was a drunk Virgil had sobered up for the occasion. He would remain sober till they got back to Leavenworth. Then they'd lock him up with a few bottles and forget him.

They tied the flattie fore and aft, put some planks down, and led the horses aboard. It took only a few minutes.

But it took two days to pole the flatboat to Hilgard. It seemed to find every mud flat in the river, to ram itself into. They invented new swear words unramming it.

However, Bill was right. It was easy to remain anonymous on the boat. No one would see them on the road leading to Hilgard—and remember them.

They tied up to the bank when they could see the rooflines of the town in the distance, and left the flattie behind. Virgil led them and the four spare horses south, away from the town, moving across country. When he thought he'd come eight or ten miles, he found a copse of trees and they tied the four.

Then they walked the other horses back to Hilgard. Outside of town they made camp by a stream, having seen no one all afternoon. Virgil had a silver windup watch.

"The bank opens at ten in the morning. We'll just be comin' into town, taking it nice and easy. We go in the bank and Dewey and Jud gets the safe open while me and

Eli stays by the door. If folks comes in, we put 'em in one of the rooms. We put the money into sacks and get the hell out." He looked at them. "Ever'body unnerstand?" As they nodded, he pointed a finger. "And no shooting. That'll just wake the town up."

"What if they shoots at us?" Eli said.

"Then you can shoot back. The thread's off the bobbin then." Virgil held up his hand. "One more thing—none of that damn paper money."

They all smiled.

It went like clockwork. They rode into Hilgard, arriving as the bank opened. They went inside with drawn guns, met no resistance, and came away with four bags filled with eagles and assorted coins. They were halfway out of town before the alarm was sounded.

A pursuit was quickly organized. The four robbers had a five-minute start and rode like the wind to the copse of trees. In minutes the saddles were swapped, and they were off again on fresh horses.

The posse never caught a glimpse of them.

★

Chapter 15

The four robbers rode into Leavenworth at night as Bill had ordered. They went to the Roden Theater and Bill received them in a back room . . . and counted the haul on a big oak table. There was a trifle less than three thousand dollars in coins.

Bill allowed each man a bonus of a hundred dollars from the loot.

When the aides had gone, Bill told Virgil, "Your boys did real good. Did anybody see you?"

"Our faces was covered."

"Good. You be sure to tell 'em not to talk about it."

"I will."

Bill smiled at the stacks of coins. "Now, the next thing is to find Preacher."

Cal Bates rode with them to Bunting's trading post, a small community on a bend of the Kansas River. Johnny Bunting greeted Cal, and his eyes widened at sight of Jessie. He said what so many had said before him: "I ain't seen a blond woman in a coon's age."

Cal told him, "We didn't ride out here to listen to your troubles."

Johnny laughed. "Lookin' at a perty woman is trouble?" He motioned, "Come on in out of the wind." He yelled to one of the boys standing around staring at them. "Put them hosses in the corral, boy."

Inside, the big trading post smelled of coal oil, tobacco, and spices. Johnny set out glasses and poured into them.

"This here's a occasion, Cal. What brings you thisaway?"

"Guns."

Jessie smiled. "More to the point, Mr. Bunting, gun-runners."

"Call me Johnny. Gunrunners? You talkin' about hombres sellin' guns to the tribes?"

"Yes, we are."

Johnny held up his glass and looked at the amber liquor thoughtfully. He said softly to Jessie and Ki, "If Cal brought you all out here, then you c'n be trusted." He glanced around. "My wife is a Sioux—and she hears things. She even tells me some of them." He smiled. "I can tell you a few things . . ."

Jessie said, "We want to know about a man called Preacher."

Johnny nodded. "I know about him. He runs with a feller called Esek. Don't know last names. They works outa Leavenworth and they been selling guns to Running Wolf."

"Where, in Leavenworth?"

"I dunno." Johnny shook his gray head. "I've just about told you all I can."

"Where do they meet Running Wolf?"

"I don't know."

"Where do they get their guns?"

"I don't know. Buy 'em here and there, I spect. Don't ask me nothing more. Runnin' Wolf hasn't raided here yet, but he might if he thought I was talkin' too much."

"We appreciate what you've said, Johnny," Jessie told him. "It helps to make it certain that Preacher is the one we want."

"He's good and bad. Good to the Sioux and bad for the whites." He drank down the liquor and sighed. "Running Wolf's got him a powerful ambition." He glanced around again. "I think he's bit off more'n he can chew. But so far his medicine has been good."

Jessie said, "The whole thing must put you in the middle . . ."

"It does that, something fierce. Running Wolf's gathering his strength. He's hit a lot of small holders, scattered buildings and some wagons. He's had to build hisself a reputation as a war leader so the young men will join him."

Cal said, "He's certainly doing that."

"Yeah, but look at it from his angle. He has to keep the young hellions fired up and believing in his power—his medicine. So most of all he has to get his hands on guns . . . and more guns. Most Indians don't yet know how to handle guns so they bust 'em up too fast. Running Wolf's big headache is getting shooters."

"We appreciate what you've told us, Johnny," Jessie said.

"I never told you nothing." He grinned. "I'll swear to it on a stack of Bibles."

Cal said, "Is there one single Bible in this entire trading post?"

"Bible?" Johnny said. "What's that?"

They returned to Leavenworth the next day and discovered that someone in government had finally dug his head out of the sand. Newspaper headlines proclaimed that a State of Readiness existed along the frontier. The cavalry was out in force. Even infantry regiments were being shipped west. The Indian problem had hit Washington City at last.

Cavalry patrols were thicker than warts on a Democrat. Every traveler on the plains was halted, questioned, and escorted to his destination or sent back. Traffic on the plains was definitely curtailed. There were breaches to be sure, but a gunrunner would have his entire load confiscated and himself put into prison—if he were caught.

It was not a profitable or even a sensible risk.

One of Cal Bates's informants decided he could double his take if he worked for both sides. It was not a fine moral judgment for him to make, since he was already the lowest of the low, an informer. His name was Jules Leach, a professional sneak.

Bates had asked him to find out what he could about the man Preacher. He wondered why Bates wanted to know, so he nosed into Bates's affairs and discovered a blond beauty and a man called Ki, a Chinaman. Since Bates was devoting all his time to the two, they must be the ones.

He redoubled his efforts looking for the preacher, and discovered him drinking in a saloon, but not delivering his sermons.

It was no trick to follow the preacher home.

He then sent Preacher a note, asking for money and offering information. He met Preacher at night, received a gold eagle, and told him about the blond woman and the Chinaman, saying the two were trying to bring the law down on him, Preacher.

Preacher said, "Where can I find them?"

"They living at the Adlam Hotel. That's all I know, Preacher."

Preacher nodded and let him go.

To Esek he said, "Why you figger they trying to git the law on us?"

"Izzat sneak tellin' the truth?"

Preacher shrugged. "He said they know we's selling guns. That ain't a good thing f'them to know. But why are *they* doin' it? Why not the law?"

"They'll turn us over to the law when they catch us."

"Damn peculiar," Preacher muttered. "Like they was vigilantes."

"Maybe that one ain't a Chinaman. Maybe he's an Indian."

"Does that make any sense?"

Esek made a face. "What you want to do about it?"

"We ought to discourage 'em. Whyn't you go look that hotel over tomorra? Maybe it'll give us an idea."

"All right."

The Adlam was an older hotel, a frame building that had seen better days but was struggling to keep up appearances.

It was a comfortable place, which was why Jessie liked it. There was none of the stiff formality of some of the newer hostelries. It had a very good restaurant and there were shops convenient.

Cal Bates came by the hotel daily to tell them what he could. The Preacher was in Leavenworth, he was certain, but the man was no longer haranguing tipplers in the saloons, and unfortunately there were other preachers in the town, some of whom did the same thing. It was his experience, Cal said, that men who took up the preaching dodge were usually poor and looked for a dollar wherever they could.

He had not yet turned up one who had a friend named Esek.

He said to Jessie, "I suspect he's lying low because of the cavalry. He and Esek can't do any dealing with Indians. It takes a wagon to haul guns and they probably don't dare risk getting through the patrols. If they're caught they'll go to prison for sure."

They were in her room, sitting on the narrow settee together, and he took her hand. "If I find this pair for you, will you go out with a six-gun to capture them?"

She laughed. "Ki and I will get the law to do it. We want to bring them to justice . . . if that's possible. If it happens that the law can't do it somehow, then yes, we will capture them."

"And if they fight?"

"They killed my father's friend. They will not go free."

He said earnestly, "I don't like to think of you, confronting an experienced killer!"

"It's sweet of you to worry, but I will be all right."

"Because of Ki?"

"Yes, and because of myself." She thought of something that Ki had asked her to do once or twice. She said, "Clap your hands."

"What?"

"Clap your hands." She showed him what she meant.

He looked puzzled. "Why?"

"Humor me. Clap your hands."

He shrugged and brought his palms together—then looked down in amazement to find her revolver between them. "My God! How did you do that!?"

"It's a trick that Ki taught me." She put the gun away. "So you see, I'm not entirely helpless."

"My God, no! You scare me a little!"

She smiled and kissed him. "No need to be—unless you preach in saloons."

He held up his hand. "I promise never to do that."

His arms slid about her and they kissed. She embraced him and they fell back. A single candle was glowing in the room, its flame like a tiny spear of light. She tugged at his shirt and helped him pull it off over his head. His boots fell to the floor, and she began to unfasten her dress as he pushed off his jeans.

He smiled as he watched the delicate way she slipped out of her outer garments and chemise, revealing ripe, round breasts. They crawled onto the bed together, and he ran his hand down her back, fondling her velvety round bottom. Then she pulled him eagerly, and he slid atop her as she guided him. Her legs tightened about his body, and she gasped, taking a long breath. He moved over her, thrusting gently, deeply . . . She moaned, kissing him . . .

And in a few minutes she panted with his thrusts, beginning to move wildly, rubbing her heels on his back . . .

★

Chapter 16

"It's a three-story hotel," Esek reported. "They on the second floor, not in the same room. They's a restaurant downstairs and a big stable in the back. The hotel's on a busy street and the stable's on a alley."

"They got a stableman?"

"Yep. But he's an old feller, lives above the stable. You figger we can bushwhack 'em there?"

"It sounds like the best place, don't it?"

"How'll we know when they goes for their horses?"

Preacher frowned. He took a turn about the kitchen. "What if we write them a note? Sign it with the stableman's name."

"You mean that something's happened to one of their horses?"

Preacher nodded. "Won't they go see?"

"Yeah, one of 'em will. Probably."

"Then that'll make it easier to git the other one."

"I don't know the stableman's name."

"Just sign it 'Stableman.' You write the best hand, Esek. Tell 'em that one of the horses is gone lame."

Esek found a scrap of paper and sat at the table, pushing the coffee cups aside. He bit his tongue and wrote laboriously.

Preacher looked out the window. "It's plenty dark out. Let's go to the hotel, soon's you finish that."

While they were getting dressed, there was a knock at the door. Cal moved aside, to where he could not be seen, and

Jessie pulled a wrap about her bare shoulders. She opened the door; a boy stood there with a note.

"F'you, ma'am."

She thanked him and took it. Leaning against the closed door, she read it and frowned.

Cal asked, "What's the matter?"

"It's from the stableman. He says one of our horses is lame. That's very odd . . ."

"Probably a worn shoe. You finish dressing. I'll go down and tell him to replace the old shoe. I'll meet you in the restaurant."

"All right."

He took the note, kissed her, and went out.

It was very dark behind the hotel as he went down the back steps and across to the stable. A lantern was burning just inside the door. He could see the light through the cracks.

He opened the door and stepped inside—and the shots came loud—very loud—

Preacher put his gun away and hurried to the body. The man had fallen facedown, crumpled against the half-open door. Preacher pulled the face around and stood up swearing.

"That's not one of 'em! He ain't a Chinaman!" He looked at the other man. "We shot the wrong man, Esek!"

"But he got the note!"

He had indeed. Preacher saw it on the ground.

Esek pulled at him. "Le's git outa here!"

They ran to the alley door, hearing yells from the hotel. Two streets over, they ducked into a saloon and sat in a corner, sipping beer.

Preacher said, "How come him to have our note?"

"I got no idea. But now they'll be warned, huh?"

"I don't figger it. He didn't have no slant eyes!"

Esek sighed. "It wasn't our night, Preacher."

"It sure wasn't." Preacher shook his head moodily. "It sure wasn't."

* * *

Jessie seated herself in the restaurant to wait. There had been a shot while she'd been on the stairs, and some commotion in the back. Maybe Cal had tarried there to see what had happened, to bring her the news.

Then surprisingly, Ki came to the table and sat opposite her, his face troubled. She said, "You look odd—what's the matter?"

"It's Cal . . ."

She felt herself go tense. "What about Cal?"

"Just a few minutes ago—he was shot in the stable."

Icy fingers gripped her. "Oh my God—is he dead?"

Ki nodded. "Someone shot him as he opened the door. He had a note that said his horse was lame—but he doesn't have a horse in the stable."

Jessie closed her eyes and gritted her teeth. "That was my note. Someone wanted me or you to come to the stable."

"Preacher!"

She nodded. "It must be."

"They wanted to kill one of us and killed Cal instead! That means they know who we are."

"I'm afraid so." She rose. "I don't feel like eating—I'm going up to the room."

He escorted her and left her at the door.

How had Preacher found out who they were? Ki sighed and rubbed his chin. Of course they had left a trail—a trail of questions. Someone they had questioned had informed Preacher. It was probably that simple.

The hunted had become the hunters.

Preacher and Esek sat at the kitchen table chewing tough beef, drinking coffee. It was very late evening.

Esek said, "There's no way we can get the guns to Runnin' Wolf. Not with the damn cavalry ever'where."

"He knows it. He'll just lay low till the army goes away. What else?"

"You figger we ought to go out to Bear Rock?"

101

"What for? To tell 'im what he already knows?"

Esek grunted. "I'm thinkin' about all them gold eagles we seen. Jesus! That was a perty sight!" He took a long breath, his thoughts flowing toward New Orleans.

"Well, the cavalry can't hang out there forever. They'll git tired when nothing happens. Then we can deliver them guns."

Esek looked around. "You hear something?"

"What?"

The back door opened and Big Bill Yellen walked in. Two men behind him paused at the door. Bill said, "Where the hell you been, Preacher?"

Preacher got up, annoyed. "I thought we was friends, Bill! How come you pushin' your way in here?"

Bill smiled with half his face. "Sure, we're friends, Preacher. Where you been?" He frowned at Esek. "Who's this here?"

"Name's Esek Kite. What you want, Bill?" There was menace in the room suddenly, though no guns were drawn. "We's peaceable folks."

Bill indicated Esek. "He know about our deal?"

Esek nodded, and Preacher said, "Sure, he knows. Him 'n' me, we're old friends."

Yellen gazed at Esek a moment. "You ain't sold them guns to nobody else?"

"Course not, brother!" Preacher looked pained.

Esek said, "We been away, visitin' a sick relative, that's all."

Bill frowned at him, but finally managed a smile. "We made us a deal, Preacher."

"I know it. You got the money?"

Bill nodded.

"In hard money?"

Bill's face clouded. "Yeah, gold, Not that damned bank paper. I keep m'word, Preacher."

"All right. How you want to work this?"

"You bring me the guns, I give you the money."

102

Preacher sat down again, pointing to a chair. Bill put his foot up on it. Preacher said, "We wasn't expecting you so soon, brother. First I got to get word to my friend that you definite wants the guns and got the cash. How many you want?"

"A hundred."

"Jesus!" Preacher said. "Oh, pardon me, brother. That's two thousand dollars!"

Bill offered a greasy smile. "I figgered for that kind of money I get a discount."

Preacher considered. "Ummm, maybe. I got to ask. Me bein' in the middle of this here deal, I can't say for sure. Give me a few days. Then I'll come to the theater."

"You said that before."

"Well, we was away visitin', like Esek said."

"All right. I want t'see the guns before I put the money down."

"I'll bring a sample."

Bill frowned. "How I know the sample is like the rest of 'em?"

Preacher rose and lifted his right hand in a solemn gesture. "I'm a man of God, brother. I swear t'you they ain't any larceny here."

"What's larceny mean?"

"Nothin' crooked."

Bill grunted, frowned at Esek again, and nodded. He turned toward the door and paused, looking back. "You come to the theater, Preacher."

"I will. Peace, brother."

Bill went out, slamming the door. Preacher fell into a chair, blowing his breath out in a long sigh. He stared at Esek. "He found out where we live."

"Yea." Esek put his elbows on the table. "I sure don't like the slant of them gents, Preacher. You really think you can trust Bill Yellen?"

"About as far as I can lift a mule. What we gonna do, Esek?"

"Well, we can sell him a hunnerd guns. That ought to keep him quiet, huh? Has he got two thousand dollars?"

"Hell, I dunno. He says he got it."

Esek frowned, and bit his lower lip hard. "What if we take and hide two crates, that's forty guns, down along the river . . . so he'll think they come from the other side. We'll tell 'im your friend will only give us a few at a time. Make Bill think he can get more, so he won't cheat us right off."

Preacher smiled. "That might work, Esek!"

"Sure it'll work. He wants guns bad, I could see it. So maybe next time we give him sixty guns . . . as long's he pays over the money."

Preacher got up and made sure the door was shut tight. "Let's hide them crates tonight. Then I'll go see Bill tomorra, late. He'll think we want to work with him."

Esek nodded. "I be glad to get shut of them guns."

It took an hour to lift down two crates and put them into one of the buckboards without making any sounds. They stretched a canvas over them, hooked up a mule, and drove to the river, well outside the town.

They hid the crates, well covered with leaves and branches, under two oaks and marked one with a hatchet. Then they drove home.

Late the next afternoon Preacher went to the Roden Theater and met Bill. Bill pulled him into a corner immediately. "You got the guns?"

Preacher nodded. "I got forty guns. That's all they would give me this time."

"Forty! I said one hunnerd!"

"Lissen, Bill, they trustin' me. I never give em a cent for the forty guns! I told 'em you want a hunnerd, but they ain't gonna trust me for all that much!"

Bill grunted, his little yellow eyes glowing.

"They got more guns, Bill. But you got to play their game."

Bill sighed deeply. "All right. You say you got 'em? Where is they?"

"They're hid where you can pick 'em up. Where's the money?"

Bill seemed to consider, then he said, "Come on." He led Preacher into another small room and closed the door. There were some guns on a shelf and an iron safe in a corner.

"You said forty guns?"

"That's eight hunnerd dollars."

Bill growled something under his breath, reached into the safe, and pulled out a heavy leather sack. He poured coins onto a small table. "You take six hunnerd?"

"Their rock bottom figger was six hunnerd. Don't I get a commission? I done all this work . . ."

Bill sighed. "Seven hunnerd then. That suit you?"

"Thanks, brother." He watched Bill count out seven hundred dollars and push it across the table.

"Count it."

Preacher counted it and nodded. Bill gave him a cloth sack and he dumped the coins in.

"How many more rifles they got?"

"They won't tell me. You want more?"

"Another sixty anyways." Bill went to the door. "Where do I go for the guns?"

Preacher explained about the oaks and the hatchet mark. Bill nodded. He said, "When I get more rifles?"

"As soon's I can get to talk to m'friend. I'll try to see 'im tomorra."

Bill nodded again.

★
Chapter 17

Cal Bates's death affected her immensely. It was such an unexpected shock; he had been so alive! And then in an instant he was gone. Jessie felt miserably responsible, and Ki could not, for a time, talk her out of the mood. After all, Cal had gone to do an errand for her . . . and had been shot.

But it strengthened her resolve to see Preacher and his companion brought to justice.

"They won't escape," Ki promised. "The shooting means they're nearby. We had feared for a time that they'd left the area . . ."

She sighed. "I wish we knew more about the other one, Esek."

"Apparently he doesn't go along when Preacher delivers his saloon sermons. At least, no one's mentioned seeing him." Ki smiled. "I'm not much of a saloon denizen. I doubt if I could spend days and days sitting in saloons watching for him . . ."

"How many saloons do you think there are in town?"

Ki rolled his eyes. "Dozens. From dirty little deadfalls to the big flashy saloon dance halls and gambling palaces. He could he in any one of them."

"And a different one every day."

"Probably. And we have to assume they're not trading with the Indians, because of the cavalry patrols—so are they trading with others? Maybe they've gone out of the gun business and are selling something else."

"Or simply stealing."

"Yes. There's always that."

"So where do we begin?"

Ki shrugged. "I have no idea."

An hour after dark Big Bill Yellen appeared at the house with two henchmen. He walked into the kitchen, where Preacher and Esek were sitting with coffee.

Preacher rose. "Hello, Bill. Wasn't the guns there?"

"Yeah, they was." Bill pulled out a chair and sat down at the table across from them. "Like you said, they good guns too. Henrys."

Preacher smiled. "Fine, brother."

Bill hunched over the table. "You all know where them guns came from?" He looked from one to the other, seeing only innocence.

"We never even seen them guns, Bill."

"They was stole out of a warehouse right here in town. Right here!" Bill's finger stabbed down on the table. "It was in the papers. Don't you read?"

"A warehouse here in town!?" Preacher was aghast. He looked at Esek, who was wide-eyed. "I'll be damned!"

"They got numbers stamped on 'em," Bill said ominously.

Preacher raised his voice. "I tole you, we never seen them guns! I tole you that from the start. I was actin' for somebody else."

"How you figger they was stole?" Esek asked.

"Because they're Henry rifles, .44-caliber, just like the paper said, twenty to a box."

"So what's the problem?" Esek asked reasonably. "Don't they shoot?"

Bill stared at him and Preacher spread his hands. "You want to give the guns back, Bill?"

"Lissen, Preacher!" Bill's voice turned hard. "I tell you what I want. They was three hundred and sixty guns in that warehouse and I want 'em all!"

"All of 'em? That's a lot of money, Bill."

"I got the damn money! You tell them friends of yourn I want the rest of the rifles." Bill reached across the table and touched Preacher lightly. "You tell 'em."

"Sure I will. Sure I will, Bill." Preacher rose as Bill got up. "I never thought they had so many."

At the door Bill said, "You bring me word tomorra."

"I'll bring it soon's I can, Bill."

Yellen nodded and went out. Preacher crossed the room and locked the door. He let his breath out and looked at Esek. "That's like bein' in the same room with a live volcano."

"I hope he believes what we tole him," Esek said.

Bill Yellen went out to his horse, and Virgil Cloud came up beside him. Bill said, "What's in the stable?"

"Nothin' but a couple buckboards, two mules, and two horses. Nothin' in the wagons."

Bill poked his chest. "You stay here for a while. Keep an eye on the house. That Preacher's got shifty eyes. No tellin' what he's up to." He climbed onto the horse.

Virgil nodded.

A few minutes after Bill Yellen left, Esek slid out to the stable and climbed to the loft in the dark. With his hands he examined the knots on the tarpaulin. No one had disturbed it. He climbed down again.

Without a lantern the loft was practically invisible. Satisfied, he returned to the house. Preacher said, "You figger he's watching us?"

"He might be."

"If he is, we can't get the gun boxes to the river. If he finds out they're here, he'll come and take 'em, sure as shootin'. We's in a bind, Preacher."

Preacher poured out more coffee and sat for several minutes, staring into the cup. "It only takes one to watch a house."

"You got an idee?"

"What about this?" Preacher turned to face the other man. "We load one of the buckboards with straw or any damn thing, tie a canvas over it, and you drive somewhere—it don't matter where—just so the watcher follers you."

Esek grinned. "While you take the guns over to the river."

"That's right. Give me two hours t'do 'er and git back."

"What if they stop me? What the hell am I doin' drivin' around in the dark?"

Preacher frowned and sipped the coffee. "You going to meet a gal. But her husband is home so you're drivin' around wondering what to do about her. How's that?"

Esek nodded. "It'll do. Let's go load the guns."

They were getting expert at loading the boxes without noise, in the dark. They loaded four boxes into a buckboard and tied the tarpaulin tight over them. Then they piled loose straw into the other wagon and pulled a canvas over it. Esek hooked up a mule and drove out to the street, making as much clatter as he could without seeming to. He headed south along a road that paralleled the open prairie, letting the mule take him as he puffed a cigar.

Several times, in the deep shadows of bordering trees, he glanced back and was able to make out the form of a single figure on a horse, following a long way behind.

Preacher had stood in the unlighted parlor, watching the street as Esek drove away. He saw the figure detach itself from the shadows and follow.

He rushed to the stable and turned the mule's head in the opposite direction. He left the four gun boxes in the same place, well hidden, and slapped the reins to get back in a hurry.

Esek came in nearly an hour later. He had stopped at a hotel on the far side of town, he told Preacher. "Like I was meetin' somebody there. I went upstairs and sat there for a long while, long enough for somebody to look in the wagon. Then I come down and drove home."

"That was good thinkin'," Preacher approved. "We fooled 'em this time, but it might not be easy again."

"What you got in mind?"

"We got to find another place for them rifles."

Esek sighed and nodded.

Bill Yellen said, "One of 'em drove across town to a hotel? What for?"

"I dunno. He went in and stayed for a while, then come out and drove home. Guess he saw somebody."

"What was in the wagon?"

"Nothin'."

"That's all? He drove there and home again? Why'd he take the wagon?"

Virgil shrugged. "I got no idea. He give the mule a lot of exercise."

Bill scowled. "In the middle of the goddam night?"

"I'm tellin' you what happened, Bill."

"All right." Bill waved him out. People did curious things. He was sitting in his shack on the edge of town. He fished for a cigar. Why would one of them make a trip at night unless it was something to do with the guns? But Preacher was the go-between, not the other one.

Had Preacher been wise to Virgil? Had the other one, Esek, led Virgil on a wild goose chase while Preacher saw the people who had the rifles? Bill snapped his thick fingers. That was possible!

Maybe the people who had the guns were known to him—or maybe they were just very damn cautious, so they dealt through Preacher. He could understand that. Bill looked at the glowing end of the cigar. So far Preacher had done what he'd said. He did look shifty as hell though . . .

The next day Preacher went to the saloon-theater and into a room with Big Bill. He drew a quick map, explaining about the two oaks and the hatchet mark again,

"They brought the guns from across the river, Bill."

"How many?"

"Four boxes. Eighty guns."

"I told you, I want 'em all!"

Preacher sighed. "Easy, brother. They trustin' me for each delivery. I getting as many as I can for you. They ain't my guns. Matter of fact, I'm surprised they let me have eighty—with nothing down. You'll git 'em all if ever'body deals fair."

Bill grumbled. "All right." He poured coins onto the table. "You take fourteen hunnerd for the lot?"

"Sure. Fourteen hunnerd for the guns and a hunnerd for me."

Bill growled, a low rumble under hid breath. "You didn't do a damn thing, Preacher! All you done was to tell 'em to put the guns by the river. How about fifty?"

"Peace, brother. I damn well earned the hunnerd. If I didn't tell 'em to put the guns there—and swear to them that you'd pay for them—you wouldn't have no guns at all. They trustin' *me,* Bill."

Bill blew out his breath. "All right. When do I get the rest of 'em?"

"I got to go ask."

Bill looked unhappy, but he counted out fifteen hundred dollars and pushed the stacks across the table. "Count it."

Preacher shook his head. "I trust you, Bill." He swept the coins into a cotton sack. Bill picked up the remaining coins and dropped them into the leather pouch, then took the pouch to the safe. Preacher got a quick look. There was another pouch there, hopefully as full.

Bill had the money all right.

He was surprised when Bill reached to take a bottle off a shelf, looked critically into two glass tumblers, and poured into them. He pushed one across the table.

"We doing a right smart lot of business, Preacher. Here's t'your health."

"Thanks, Bill." They clinked glasses. Preacher sipped the whiskey, not bad stuff. Bill surprised him further by offering a cigar. He took it and Bill supplied a match.

"Sit down for a minute, Preacher. You ain't in any hurry . . ."

"Esek's waitin' out in the wagon."

"Let 'im wait for a minute." Bill puffed his cigar. "These friends o'yourn. They got any guns besides these here Henrys?"

"I dunno. I got to ask."

"How about ammunition?"

Preacher shrugged. "I dunno."

"Swords?"

"I dunno that either. All's I heard about was the Henry rifles."

"Where'd you meet 'em?"

"Long time ago." Preacher waved his arm vaguely. Why the hell was Bill asking him all these questions? He said, "What you going to do with the guns, Bill?"

"Use 'em in a good cause."

"What cause is that, brother?"

"I ain't at liberty t'tell you." Bill finished the whiskey and looked at Preacher's glass. "Drink up. They's more here."

Preacher finished the glass and stood up. "I got to be going, Bill. Thanks."

"You see me tomorra."

"I will. Peace, brother." Preacher went out to the wagon, feeling vaguely uneasy. He had never seen Bill smile before. He felt like the lamb, when the lion said, "It'll all be over in a second. You won't feel a thing."

When he got in, Esek slapped the reins. "You got the money?"

"Yeah. Let's go home."

Esek stared at him. "What's the matter? He give you trouble?"

"No. And maybe *that's* the trouble. He didn't argue hardly at all, just the usual growls like he always does." Preacher sighed deeply. "I wish we was back dealing with Runnin' Wolf."

"No way we can do that now. Let's us find a place to hide them guns and see if we can unload all of 'em to somebody. But not to Bill Yellen."

"What if he finds out?"

Esek made a face. "I dunno. We cross that bridge when we come to it."

"Perty dangerous. Perty damn dangerous."

They said nothing more till they reached the house. Esek turned into the yard, and Preacher got down to open the stable doors. He stared, then yelled, "The wagon's gone!"

Esek jumped off the seat. A mule was missing too. He climbed up to the loft. The tarpaulin that had been tied around the rifle crates was gone—and so were the crates.

He looked down at Preacher. "We been robbed!"

★

Chapter 18

Chief Deputy Simon Strater stood up as Jessie entered the office, followed by Ki. Strater smiled and indicated chairs. "It is always a pleasure to look up and find a beautiful woman in my doorway."

Jessie laughed, taking a chair. "Such flattery will get you a lunch at your convenience . . ."

Strater nodded. "I accept. I suppose you're here to talk about Preacher?"

"Have you learned anything at all?"

The lawman shrugged. "The trouble is, we haven't any evidence against him. Nothing that would hold up in court. If I arrested him, his lawyer would have him out the same day."

Ki said, "We're certain he was behind the murders and robbery at Hitchens Armory."

"I believe you. But would a court? There is no evidence at all that I know of."

Jessie frowned. "There's the watch—I mean Private Larson's watch . . ."

Strater nodded. "Yes, we know about that, of course, but again, there's no evidence that Preacher has it. And we can't find Preacher to ask him."

"The watch was missing when the body was discovered," Ki said. "Presumably the killer has it."

Strater replied, "If Preacher was the killer, the chances that he kept the watch are very slim."

"It was apparently a very expensive watch," Jessie said. "He might have."

114

Ki agreed. "Sometimes long shots pay off."

"Yes, they do, thank goodness," Jessie said.

Virgil Cloud had looked into the stable as soon as he saw Preacher and Esek go to see Bill Yellen. Bill had ordered, "Give the house and stable a good goin' over. I don't trust them two. If they's nothing in either one, look to see if they been digging in the yard."

He didn't have to look any farther than the stable. In daylight he noticed the loft at once, and climbed up. Twelve crates of guns! He shouted down to Jud Walsh, and the two of them wrestled the crates down and loaded them into the buckboard, hooked up a mule, and drove away.

They drove directly to the river, laid down planks, and pushed the buckboard onto a flatboat. Then Jud hurried away to the theater to tell Bill.

Bill was lolling in a big chair, drinking whiskey with Preacher. When the visitor's head was turned, Jud made a sign to Bill, who nodded.

A few minutes later, Preacher left the building.

The door was hardly closed behind him when Jud said, "We got the guns, Bill! Twelve crates! They was in the stable loft."

"That lyin' son of a bitch!" Bill yelled, smacking the door. "That goddam Bible-spouting bastard!"

"We got the guns, Bill . . ."

Bill controlled his anger. "All right." He gave a look around and took a long breath. "There's nothin' here I want. Let's go."

They went down to the horses.

But it was disgusting—Preacher standing up to him with the story about having to talk to somebody else, when he had the guns all the goddam time! Bill deplored such treatment. Especially when he had dealt fair with Preacher and given him mostly what he wanted for the rifles.

They poled the flattie into the stream and headed toward Kansas City, not far off. Bill had contacts there.

But he had one more chore to do. With furrowed forehead, he wrote out a letter addressed to the Leavenworth police, accusing the Preacher and Esek of stealing the Henry rifles from the Therry & Son warehouse. He told the police where to find the culprits.

The letter was posted across the Missouri at the first town, and the flatboat continued downriver.

Upon receipt of the letter, the police immediately surrounded the house and took Preacher into custody.

However they missed grabbing Esek Kite. He was not in the house at the time and returned to see lawmen everywhere. He joined other gawkers and watched Preacher being hauled away.

The police went through the house and stable, looking for evidence, and found no guns. But one of the searchers noticed some nails that had recently been hammered into the stable wall; the rust was off the nail heads. When the boards were pulled away, a cache of jewels in leather pouches was discovered.

In the station house the jewelry was laid out and examined—rings, watches, necklaces, brooches . . . many with names and inscriptions.

Someone thought to compare the names with the names of people killed in Indian raids.

Many of them matched.

Preacher was then charged with receiving these items from the Indians in payment for weapons.

He was put into a small room and questioned by a stocky policeman. "You been dealing with Running Wolf?"

"Who's that?"

"He's an Indian. He give you all this jewelry, huh? How many guns you sell him?"

"I never sold nobody any guns."

"You sold him the guns from the Hitchens Armory."

Preacher was outraged. "I did not!"

"Where'd you get the watch belongin' to William Larson?"

116

"I bought it in a saloon."

"Where are the Henry rifles you stole from the warehouse?"

"I never stole no rifles! If I stole 'em—where are they?"

"I just asked you that."

"I never stole no guns."

"Where's Esek Kite?"

"I don't know. Him and me split up."

"You're a liar, Preacher."

"Peace, brother. You can't prove nothing."

The policeman went out of the room and discussed the case with others. No guns had been found; maybe the letter was wrong. Maybe someone had it in for the preacher.

More likely, another cop said, the preacher had already sold the guns.

Deputy Strater asked, "Who searched Preacher? What did you find?"

They had found five hundred dollars on him. Strater asked, "Where did he get it?"

"He said he passed the hat in saloons when he preached the gospel."

"He got five hundred from that? He's a liar." Strater was annoyed. "I want five men to go back and search that house and stable again. Look for money. I'm convinced he's sold the Henry rifles. Remember, we're dealing with a very slippery article."

The men returned to the house. They took it apart but found only one hundred and fifty dollars in a jar in the kitchen. Nothing else.

Jessie and Ki visited the jail, and Deputy Strater took them back to look at the man they'd sought so long. As described, he was tall and dour-looking, and he refused to talk or to answer questions.

In his office, Strater said, "We thought both of them were in the house when we surrounded it, but the other one, Esek, eluded us. His name's Esek Kite, by the way. I've got men out now, looking for him."

Jessie said, "The newspapers have tried and convicted them both of robbing the warehouse."

"Yes, I know. But we have no evidence on that score, unfortunately. We're sure they did it, but we can't prove it." He smiled, "But the watch is going to convict him, I'm sure."

"Larson's watch . . . ?"

"Yes. We think he was used to carrying it and had forgotten the inscription inside. Myself, I think he couldn't resist it, a valuable watch like that. He should have put it with the other jewels."

"Do you think he'll implicate Esek?"

Simon nodded. "I'm sure of it. Crooks like Preacher aren't the kind to protect a companion in crime. I'm sure he'll never be able to see Esek go free while he gets the rope. He'll talk."

Jessie sighed. "Let's hope so."

"Yes. And there's one other thing."

"What?"

"We still have to catch Esek."

Preacher was taken to Hitchens to stand trial for murder. Four men took him in a heavily constructed wagon with steel bars, and put him in a cracker-box jail, on a side street in the little town, to await the judge.

Esek followed them, well out of sight.

Hitchens was a small town; it had been twice the size when the armory was employing several hundreds, but now the population had dwindled. The town was still the county seat, however, and had an old, weathered courthouse, used perhaps half the year. The lawyers and judges preferred to use the newer one at Lindon, fifty miles away. Lindon would become the county seat in another two years, and Hitchens would be allowed to wither on the vine.

The armory had already been deserted by the army. A caretaker now lived behind the wire, and a sign proclaimed the buildings and the site for sale.

Jessie and Ki put up at the only hotel, a nine-room building in the center of town. Its accomodations, however, were hardly better than those in the jail—without the bars.

The local marshal, an elderly man named Gregory, had no deputy. "The town can't afford it," he told them. "We got no crime here. Except for an occasional drunk, the jail ain't used."

"You have a dangerous man in it now," Ki said.

"That so? Well, he can't git out. We got stout bars and them walls is two-feet thick and hard as a politician's head. Now that we got us a real prisoner, I sleep in the office on a cot."

"When is the judge likely to appear?" Jessie asked.

"Prob'ly inside two weeks. We're short on judges in the territory, and we ain't needed one here for three, four months. Mostly I just fines the drunks and lets 'em go."

There was nothing they could do in Hitchens but wait for the judge and the trial to start; there was nothing *to* do in the little town. Ki suggested they return to Leavenworth and come back when the judge had arrived.

The army had announced it would send a prosecutor to press the case since it was a soldier who had been killed.

Preacher hired a lawyer from Lindon to defend him.

Esek had his choice of a dozen abandoned shacks in Hitchens. He selected one with a small corral and a sturdy privy and took up residence. He assumed the character of a grumpy drifter who wanted no company, not an unusual thing. When someone happened to come close to his door, Esek opened it with a rifle pointed, and the visitor beat a hasty retreat. He was not disturbed again.

He investigated the jail and found it annoyingly stout, a frame outer skin over adobe with a thick tar-paper roof. It had windows on the street side and tiny little ones high up in the jail area, used only for ventilation.

Esek saw that the marshal stayed in the jail office, and a boy brought him and the prisoner food on a covered tray twice a day from the town's only restaurant.

Esek sat with a newspaper, in a chair on the main street, and watched the boy go back and forth several times. He decided that would be his plan. He'd take the boy's place one night, put a revolver in the marshal's belly, and force him to unlock Preacher's cell.

Then they would put the marshal in the cell and ride into the night.

★
Chapter 19

But as Esek was about to put his plan into effect, the circuit judge arrived. The day after, the army prosecutor, a civilian, and his young clerk came in on the stage.

As he had agreed, the marshal notified Jessie and Ki by wire, and they set out at once.

The trial was held in one of the two courtrooms in the old building. It had been swept out and dusted; oil had been poured into the lamps, and benches for the audience brought up from the basement. It was the biggest event in Hitchens since the shooting. The courtroom was crowded.

Preacher was brought into the room adorned with leg irons and handcuffs. The judge ordered the cuffs taken off, to which the prisoner said, "Thankee, brother—I mean, Your Honor."

The charge was read: The prisoner was accused of brutally murdering army Private William Larson by firing a pistol into his chest at close range.

Preacher was told to stand, and the judge asked, "How do you plead?"

His lawyer, Mr. Beech, said, "Not guilty, Your Honor."

Beech was a lanky man with a coat that apeared too small for him; his hairy wrists were not covered by the sleeves.

Preacher said loudly, "I didn't shoot nobody."

The judge stared at him. "Mr. Beech, can you manage to keep your client quiet?"

"Yes, Your Honor. Sorry." Beech hissed at Preacher.

Jessie and Ki sat to one side and had a good view of the defendant. Preacher looked more shabby than ever. He had apparently been sleeping in his clothes and had attempted to shave; his face was nicked with small wounds and looked splotchy. He was also a good deal thinner, Jessie thought.

Ki had peered at each member of the large audience, wondering if Esek would have the beans to attend—but there was no one present who resembled the description they had. Probably Esek had headed for the timberline when he'd discovered Preacher was in jail.

As the trial started, the prosecutor bore down heavily on the evidence of Private William Larson's pocket watch. The watch lay on the table in front of the bench and had a large white tag attached to it.

The prosecutor picked it up and waved it at Preacher. "This watch was in your possession when you were arrested, was it not?"

"I bought it in a saloon," Preacher said. "I never seen this Larson."

"You must have noticed the inscription inside . . ."

"The man I bought it from said that was his uncle."

"Why did he sell the watch?"

Preacher moved his shoulders. "Because he needed the money."

The prosecutor was more and more irritated by Preacher's answers. He said, "Your Honor, this man is lying. He did not buy the watch in a saloon. He took the watch off the body of his victim, Private Larson."

Preacher yelled, "Did you see me do it!?"

The judge rapped with his gavel. "Be quiet, Mr. Hanks."

Preacher demanded, "You said I killed him—why would I kill him?"

The gavel rapped harder. "Mr. Beech, please control your client."

"Yes, Your Honor." Beech pulled Preacher down into his chair, talking to him angrily.

The judge adjusted his spectacles and rattled some papers. "According to the allegation, the killer took the victim, Private Larson, a mile or more out of town to rob him and shoot him. Do you mean to prove that, Mr. Prosecutor?"

"The body of Private Larson was found that distance out of town, Your Honor. Yes."

"That's not what I asked you. How do you intend to prove Mr. Hanks did this crime? Do you have witnesses?"

The prosecutor grew red. "Ahh, no, Your Honor. But the watch—"

"Yes, the watch. I am curious about one other thing. Why do you suppose someone would take his victim a mile out of town to rob and kill him?"

"So the shot would not be heard . . ."

The judge made a face. "Have you ever heard of a thief walking his victim out into the prairie in order to rob him?"

"Well, no . . ."

"But you are asking this court to believe that!"

"Your Honor, the body was *found* there!"

"Yes, I'm prepared to believe it. But can you place the defendant, Mr. Hanks, at that precise location at the time of the shooting?"

The prosecutor sighed deeply and shook his head. "We believe there were two men involved in this robbery and murder, Your Honor. We have not yet apprehended the second man."

"Yes, I see. His name is listed as Esek Kite." The judge looked at Preacher over his spectacles. "Where is Mr. Kite?"

Preacher shrugged. "I dunno, Judge. Me and him split up a while ago."

The judge stared at him for a moment, then turned to the prosecutor. "Do you have any other evidence, sir?"

"The watch is—"

"That watch is not enough to convict anyone of murder. You have not shown the court that the accused took the watch from the person of Private Larson, alive or dead. Have you anything further?"

"Yes, Your Honor. Mr. Hanks is accused of another, even more heinous crime, that of selling guns to the hostile tribes and thereby causing the deaths of a good many persons."

The judge nodded, reading the allegation. "Please continue."

The prosecutor motioned, and two aides brought in several leather pouches and quickly dumped a glittering pile of jewelry and watches on the table in front of the bench.

His Honor leaned over, staring at the assortment. "What is this?"

"Your Honor, these items of jewelry and timepieces were found concealed in Mr. Hanks's stable. My men have determined they were placed there recently. Many of these items have names and inscriptions engraved on them. An investigation by the county sheriff has shown that many of the names match those of people killed by hostile Indians. The Indians took the items from the bodies." He pointed an accusing finger at Preacher. "These items were then given to this man as payment for guns!"

"I did not!" Preacher yelled.

There was instant hubbub in the courtroom. The judge pounded with his gavel, calling for order, threatening to clear the room. It took several minutes for everyone to settle down.

The judge said, "You say these articles were found hidden in Mr. Hanks's stable?"

"Yes, Judge."

His Honor frowned at Preacher. "How did the articles get into your stable, Mr. Hanks?"

"I got no idea, Judge. I never seen 'em before."

"I find that very difficult to believe."

"Somebody else put 'em there."

The judge looked at the papers before him. "You had five hundred dollars on your person when you were arrested, Mr. Hanks. Where did you get that money?"

"I got it gambling. I was lucky."

The prosecutor said icily, "You preach against gambling, I'm told."

Preacher said nothing. Mr. Beech rose. "Everyone gambles now and then, for God's sake. It's not a crime!"

"No, but I find that very curious because of the evidence now presented." His Honor indicated the jewelry. He regarded Preacher steadily. "Do you still maintain, Mr. Hanks, that you know nothing of these articles?"

"They ain't mine, Your Honor."

The judge regarded his papers a moment, then looked up. "I think I've seen and heard enough, Mr. Prosecutor." He stared at Preacher. "Mr. Hanks, I find you guilty of the charges leveled against you. You are ordered to return here tomorrow morning at eleven o'clock for sentencing."

His gavel came down sharply.

In the hotel Jessie said, "What's your guess? Ten years in prison for Preacher?"

Ki smiled. "Let's hope it's at least that. He deserves every day of it. But I wouldn't be surprised if they hanged him."

"Well, the court has done our job for us—except for Esek. I wish we knew more about him."

"So do I. I expect he's holed up somewhere waiting for this commotion to die down. So far Preacher hasn't shown any inclination to help us find him."

"I hope that changes . . ."

"It might—if they give Preacher the rope."

In the first saloon he visited, Esek heard the details of the trial; they were on everyone's lips. Preacher Hanks had been convicted and would be sentenced on the morrow. The guessing was he would hang for trading guns to the Indians and causing so many deaths.

The names on the jewelry items were damning evidence.

He also heard that the law was looking for the second man, Esek Kite. They had a description of him but no picture.

Esek swore under his breath. Preacher knew too much about him—he could give them important details that might aid in the search. If Preacher helped them, they'd have

125

posters out soon, plastered everywhere. And Esek was sure Preacher would do it, if he did not get him out. In a way Esek was saving his own skin.

So his first order of business was to free Preacher. And he had better do it tonight. Tomorrow, after the sentence was pronounced, they might move the prisoner to a better jail.

It was dark out, and according to his watch, the boy would deliver the food tray to the jailhouse in an hour. Esek tied his horse near the jail and went looking for another mount. He found a good-looking blue roan gelding on a side street with no one near. He stepped up into the saddle and rode to the jail, where he tied the horse next to his bay.

Then he walked across to the restaurant and waited for the boy to appear. When the lad came out, Esek accompanied him to the jail, explaining that he was the marshal's brother and had come to help the marshal celebrate his birthday.

The boy was surprised. "He didn't say nothing about it bein' his birthday!"

"That's the way he is," Esek said. "Doesn't want folks to take on about him. But I got a present for him." He slapped a pocket.

At the door the boy rapped, and the marshal called out, "Who izzit?"

"It's me, Charlie," the boy replied, and the marshal opened the barred door. And looked into Esek's revolver muzzle.

Esek said softly, "Don't do nothing foolish, Marshal."

★
Chapter 20

Esek took the marshal's gun and marched him and the boy into the cell area as the marshal protested he would not get away with this! Esek paid no attention.

Preacher sat up on his cot, seeing the new arrivals, and grinned at Esek. "I figgered you for about now . . ."

Esek shoved the marshal and the boy, who still carried the tray, into the next cell, and slammed the door. With the keys he unlocked Preacher's cell door. "Come on outa there . . ."

"They gonna hang you both!" the marshal yelled.

Preacher smiled at him. "Peace, brother," he said and went into the office, slamming the heavy door, and barring it. Preacher's pistol was hanging on a nail behind the marshal's desk. He took it and they went outside to the horses.

A mile from the town, as they headed west, Esek tossed the keys into the weeds.

The boy's parents became alarmed when he did not return home, and the father went to the jail. He found the marshal and the boy locked in a cell—and no key ring. The two had to spend the night in the jail, and a rider was sent to bring a locksmith from the next town.

The event caused a terrible uproar, and a search was instituted finally, when the marshal got out. But no one had seen the two fugitives, and it was impossible to tell which way they had gone. The search fizzled out.

No one doubted it had been Esek Kite who had engineered the jailbreak. The description of him by the marshal and the boy confirmed what everyone already knew.

Information about the two men went out on the telegraph.

Jessica and Ki returned to Leavenworth to confer with Chief Deputy Simon Strater. He had collected informaton about Esek Kite. "We've been in communication with other agencies," he told them. "We're hazy about Preacher, but Esek Kite comes from Arizona Territory. We think he might go back there to hide out."

"Does he have kin there?"

"We are sure of it. He comes from a little wide place in the road called Rincon. It's not on a telegraph line, and I guess it's in pretty wild country."

Ki glanced at Jessie. "That's a long way to go to hide out . . ."

"Well, there's a good reason for it," Strater said. "The court handed down a sentence of death by hanging in Preacher's case, so we can assume Esek Kite will get the same. That means you're up against two very dangerous men who have nothing to lose. Watch yourselves if you go after them."

When they were alone, Ki said, "Arizona Territory is at the end of the earth from here . . ."

"But it's our only lead."

"Maybe they went the other way, not west at all. We could lose two months."

"I feel it in my bones, they went back there."

Ki looked at her speculatively. Her hunches had paid off before. But it was a long, long way to go . . .

She read his mind. "It's our only lead."

They spread out a map and pored over it, tracing their route by stagecoach. Ki frowned. "Rincon isn't even on the map."

The journey looked to be about fifteen hundred miles over the plains and across the Continental Divide. It was a long way to go on a hunch, as Jessie admitted.

"But we've really no other choice. I agree they could have gone anywhere, but we ought to run down every lead."

"You sound like a detective."

She smiled. "There's detecting to be done." She looked at him. "Well, what shall we do?"

"You're right." He sighed. "We have to follow the leads. And this is the only one at the moment."

Ki had a discussion with the owner of the stable where they kept their horses and sold him both horses and saddles. Then he bought stage tickets and sturdy suitcases.

They boarded the stagecoach next morning.

It was a long, wearying trip, as they had expected. Summer had passed and fall was in the air; the nights were getting colder, especially in the mountains. They had bought greatcoats and wrapped themselves in them, but suffered occasional rains and the wind that came whistling into the coach, an icy, uninvited guest.

They were tired and bruised from the constant jolting of the stagecoaches, which had no springs, only leather braces. Their nights at the way stations became a blur of eating and sleeping, and each passed into limbo, one very like the last and all forgettable.

Several of the stage drivers, as they approached Arizona Territory, had heard of Rincon. They were told to go north from the town of Victor. All the drivers agreed on one thing. "It ain't much."

Esek was of two minds about returning to his boyhood home. It looked smaller, as they rode in, and it was shabby. He had never noticed it as a lad, but it looked poor, maybe since he could compare it to real towns as far east as the Missouri.

The house he had been born in was gone. It had burned to the ground, he was told, when someone carelessly placed a lamp and it caught curtains . . . His relatives still owned the land, however, and since the barn was still standing, he and Preacher moved into the rooms behind it and made do.

Esek went around, talking to those who remembered him, but many of the people his age had moved away or had been taken by the Lord. To those he knew, he said, "I just wanted to see the old place once more . . ."

News of the jailbreak had not reached Rincon, and might not ever. The weekly, when it arrived from Norman a week later, did not mention it. No one cared much what happened a thousand miles away . . . if it did not affect them.

But Esek and Preacher's money was running out.

"What we need," Esek said when they were alone behind the barn, "is another warehouse like that one with the Henry rifles."

"When we had 'em, you was in a dither t'get rid of 'em. You forgot that?"

"Well, we need to do something. We going to be flat in a week. Why don't we go up to Norman? It's a lot bigger burg than this."

Preacher was willing. And Norman proved to be a much larger town, on a railroad spur line. It was in the center of cattle country, with Fort Elsby five miles out of town and cavalrymen filling the bars every Saturday night.

There had been no hostile Indian action in the area for years. Cattlemen complained about losing cows to roving bands, but no houses had been torched or scalps taken.

The town had two banks. Esek and Preacher looked them over critically, and neither seemed to be especially tough nuts. Each had shotgun guards, but the guards had seen nothing alerting for years and were obviously unprepared.

There were also a few cattle dealers, and two in particular that Preacher thought were very interesting.

"They got safes full of money to pay out for cows. We ought t'be able to figger something from that."

"If we catch 'em when the safe is open."

Jessica and Ki stopped in Victor and stayed overnight. A road led north from the town, and Rincon, so the hotel manager told them, was some fifty miles northwest as the crow flew. "Probably sixty by the road."

But there was no stage to Rincon.

"If you wants to go to Norman, you go over through Bassington, which is the long way round, but the road past Rincon is only a trail and nobody uses it but owlhoots and coyotes."

It was necessary to purchase horses and equipment, and it took two days to arrive in Rincon. It was not much, as they had been told—a little cluster of houses and stores in a wide, shallow valley. It had a main street that dog-legged and petered out at both ends. There was a hotel and five saloons, three with dance halls . . . and diverting girls upstairs.

The hotel had a fine facade, but it hid a row of flimsy cell-like rooms, each with a door without locks and walls that did not go to the ceiling. The rooms had an iron cot and one chair each and pegs to hang clothes on. Travelers supplied their own bedrolls.

"A jail," Ki said, "has better fixings."

Ki asked in the saloons about Esek Kite, saying he was a friend and he'd heard Esek had come home.

Most of the answers were stares. Apparently he was not believed. He heard murmurs about the "Chinaman." He got the impression that Esek was not in town, but he also had a feeling that Esek might have said something concerning strangers asking about him.

Then the local law stopped him on the street. "You a Pinkerton, mister?"

"No. Certainly not."

"Why you askin' so many questions then?"

Ki shrugged. "I've only been asking about Esek Kite. Do you know him?"

"Course I know him. What you want him for?"

"We were friends in Leavenworth. Worked at the same place for a while. When I came this way I thought I'd look him up. That's all."

"Well, he ain't here."

"I'm beginning to realize that."

The lawman squinted. "You a Chinaman?"

"No. Half Japanese. Have you any idea where Esek went?"

The other man shook his head. "None a-tall."

"Nobody knows anything," Ki told Jessie as they stood in the stable behind the hotel. It was impossible to talk in the rooms; anything said in one could be heard in all.

"He was here, with someone who must have been Preacher, but they left at night without saying anything to anyone—so far as I can find out."

Jessie frowned. "They could be looking for something to rob . . ."

"Yes. That occured to me . . . that they might be short of cash. So they'd go to a bigger town, wouldn't they?"

She smiled. "Yes. More opportunities."

"The closest larger town is Norman."

"I was about to say the same thing."

They left in the early morning and found the road as it had been described to them—nothing more than a sketchy trail that wound through the hills like a winter creek, taking the path of least resistance.

But they saw no one, and two days later the rooflines and smoke of Norman cluttered the horizon. It was a town on the flats, surrounded on two sides by low, round hills showing considerable green since the fall rains had swept over them.

It was a much larger town than Rincon and was spread out over a wide area, with houses, barns, and shacks dotting the outskirts. The main street was wide, crowded in places by wagons and teams; there were three cross streets, and all the buildings were weathered, with faded signs. Outside the town on the north were the railroad buildings and facilities, a siding where boxcars waited, and many cattle pens and corrals, now empty.

The Bridgeman Hotel, Horace Bridgeman, Prop., seemed the best hostelry. They took adjoining rooms on the second floor, and Ki went down to the closest saloon and sipped a beer, asking the bartender if anyone had been preaching in the saloon lately.

"Nobody," the man said. "Leastways not for the year I been here."

He stopped in three other saloons along the street, and received similar answers.

He said to Jessie over supper, "Maybe he isn't passing the hat anymore."

"We assume he did it only to get money. Maybe we're wrong about them needing it."

"Yes, maybe. And maybe he and Esek aren't in this town at all. There are larger places. Coming here was just a guess."

Jessie smiled. "I still have my hunch . . ."

★

Chapter 21

They found a deserted shack on the edge of town and moved into it. It would only be for a short time, Esek said. "I got a feeling our luck is gonna turn."

They looked over the two banks carefully. One had two guards; the other, three. Both banks were close to the sheriff's office, and they noted that one deputy was always on duty. They could see him through the open door.

The getaway was important; both banks were near the center of town. If they didn't fire a shot, Esek said, they'd have a good chance of getting away before anyone realized the bank had been held up.

"Can't depend on it," Preacher said shortly. "One of them guards is liable to get excited. I figger we can clean one out and hightail it down the side street and over the near hills before they can organize a pursuit."

"You don't know how fast they can get started."

"They prob'ly gonna mill around some, shoutin' at each other. What's the matter, you worryin'?"

"I don't like it that we'd have to ride through half the goddam town."

Preacher let his breath out. "You got a better idee?"

"No . . . Let's get somethin' to eat. Can we afford it?"

"We got about forty dollars between us."

In the restaurant, Preacher finished his steak and sipped bitter coffee. He leaned closer, "What about this . . ."

"What?"

Preacher lowered his voice to a whisper. "Them banks got guards—but the cow dealers don't."

Esek nodded. "That's right."

"Let's look at them tomorra."

They started early, on a misty day that toyed with the notion of raining. One of the cattle dealers had an office very near a bank; another was upstairs across from the sheriff's office.

But the third was not far from the railroad buildings and pens in a long, once-green building. There were three offices on the ground floor. The cattle dealer, P. K. Judkins, was on the end. There were two "painless" dentists upstairs and a photographer.

Across the street was a rooming house and a grocery store, next to the Eden Saloon and Grill. There were hitch racks along the street but no horses at all. The saloon was not open that early.

Esek stared at the dealer's office. "He may got a safe in there, but how'll we know if it's open?"

"We suggest that he open it."

"Some people are stubborn as hell. It might take an hour to convince him." Esek grunted. "And then folks is liable to come in while we's doing it. It could get to be a mess."

That was true, Preacher reflected. He sat on the bench in front of the saloon and frowned at the railroad pens.

Esek said, "Why don't one of us just go over there when we gets ready and look in the office? If the safe's open, we go in."

"What if the safe's not open?"

Esek shrugged. "Then nothin's lost."

"Yes it is. He seen you look in the first time. That dealer'll wonder why you a-lookin' at the layout. The next time you go up his steps he'll have a gun in his hand. Them kinds of folks is suspicious as all get out because they got gold layin' around. We got to think of something else."

Esek sighed. They sat for several moments; then Preacher said, "I got it."

"What?"

Preacher got up and walked down to the rooming house, Esek close behind him. "What? Dammit, what?"

"I wonder if I can see into that office from up there on the second floor." He grinned at Esek and went up the steps.

There was a long hallway at the top, running from the front to the back, and there was a window overlooking the street. Preacher could see the two windows of the cattle dealer's office, but the shades were drawn. Apparently it was too early for business.

In the street he said to Esek, "We got to come here when the office is open. They got the shades drawn."

"You figger you can see in then?"

"Yeah, with a spyglass." He grinned at Esek.

"A spyglass!"

"Yeah. Let's go find one."

Later in the morning of the next day, they rode to the end of the green building, and Preacher went across the street with a pair of binoculars under his arm. He climbed the stairs to the window; there was no one in the long dusty hall. The window was grimy and he rubbed it with his sleeve; the shades were pulled on the office windows.

Focusing the glass on the dealer's office, he could see a man in shirtsleeves writing at a desk. He looked to be in his fifties. There was a gold leaf sign on the window: P. K. Judkins. This must be him.

Behind him was an open safe. Preacher saw it clearly.

He hurried down the stairs and across the street, nodding to Esek on the way. They walked the horses to the end office and wrapped the reins around the hitch pole. Esek walked to the door with a revolver down by his side. Glancing at the street, Preacher followed.

The office was square with a dark brown carpet and plum-colored chairs. To the left were two back-to-back desks with a fancy brass lantern hanging over them. The man writing looked up and started to speak—then he saw the gun and jumped to his feet, reaching into a drawer.

Esek shot him and he crumpled, knocking over the chair he'd been sitting in.

A second man yelped from a corner, and Preacher turned in surprise and pulled the trigger twice. This one was a younger man wearing a green eyeshade. His white shirt was instantly spotted with blood, and he fell over the desk as if a huge hand had pushed him. He took some papers with him to the floor and lay still.

Esek dived at the open safe, pulling out a stack of greenbacks wrapped with a paper band. He swept other papers aside, cursing; it was the only money. He shoved the bills at Preacher, who stuffed them into his pocket and went to the door to look at the street.

Esek yanked out desk drawers, but found only a few coins and ignored them. Preacher growled. "Come on— let's go. We got all they is."

Esek kicked a chair out of the way, and they ran to the horses. No one was in the street. Hadn't the shots been heard? As he mounted, Esek saw a man in a white coat at the door of the office. He had probably come from upstairs. Esek spurred after Preacher, who led around the corrals, across the railroad tracks, and into the fields beyond. They galloped the horses to the low hills and found a cattle path to the crest. They halted to look back; no one was following. "Jesus!" Esek said, "we done that slick!"

"Keep a-going," Preacher said, turning his horse. "If anybody was looking, they seen where we went."

They rode west the rest of the day, and late in the afternoon, coming on a patch of hard-packed ground, Esek in the lead turned at right angles and went south. As it got dark, they holed up under a ledge where low cliffs had been formed in ages past. There was dense brush cover, so they made a fire in a deep hole and boiled coffee. Preacher counted the money.

They had seven hundred dollars.

"Goddam!" Esek growled. "That ain't fair! He ought to have more in that safe than that!"

Preacher said philosophically, "It's better'n nothing. Yesterday we was about flat broke." He divided the greenbacks and passed half over.

"It was them corrals." Esek snarled. "We didn't watch the goddam corrals. We hit him at the wrong time, when he wasn't buying cows. They was no herd in them pens."

Preacher nodded. That was true. They should have waited. But he hadn't thought of it—he had been so pleased by his spyglass idea, he hadn't thought ahead.

Jessie and Ki had only just arrived at the sheriff's office in Norman, to talk to the deputy in charge, when the rider galloped up to say that Glen Dykes's office had been held up and Dykes and another man killed.

"How long ago?" the deputy demanded.

"Mebbe ten minutes . . ."

The deputy locked the office and sent a boy for another man, who was home, off duty. Then they hurried to the scene.

One of the dentists from upstairs, an ex-soldier, had kept gawkers out of the dealer's office until the law arrived. He was a thin man who had on a white coat over street clothes. He wore thick spectacles and had silver hair. He had seen the killers and could describe them.

"One was taller, in black clothes, dark mustache, sort of stooped. The other was shorter and stocky." He pointed. "They went around the corrals there, across the tracks and over the fields to the hills."

"Preacher and Esek," Jessie said. "The description fits."

"I heard the shots," the dentist said, "so I came downstairs—the door was open and I could see Glen lying there by the desk. I saw the two killers getting on their horses." He shrugged helplessly. "There was nothing I could do for Glen and the other one—I don't know his name. They were both dead."

The deputy looked at Jessie. "You mean Preacher Hanks and Esek Kite? I just got a flyer on them."

"Yes. Hanks was convicted of murder at Hitchens. He and Esek were in Rincon very recently. We are looking for him. That's why we came to your office a bit earlier."

Ki said, "We'd like to go along with your posse. We've seen Preacher close up."

The deputy rounded up five men with bedrolls, rifles, and food. It took an hour to get organized; then they were off, following plain tracks.

The deputy, Bob Harris, was getting on toward middle age; he had a square no-nonsense face and a heavy body. He led them at an easy lope, riding beside Jessie, asking why they were looking for the two men. She explained the circumstances. "Now that Preacher has been convicted, it makes the job a little easier, in a sense. All we want to do now is turn him over to the nearest law—along with Esek, who is just as guilty."

Harris said, "They won't give up easy. Not with that conviction hanging over their heads."

Ki moved up beside them and heard the last exchange. "We don't expect them to. How does your flyer read?"

The deputy smiled shortly. "It says Dead or Alive."

Ki nodded.

★

Chapter 22

Using the binoculars, Preacher made sure there were no telegraph wires entering the town before they rode in slowly at dusk. No one paid them any particular attention, and they got down in front of the Drover's Saloon.

Preacher slapped his hat against his leg and brushed at dusty clothes.

Esek said, "We best throw these old duds away and get us new ones."

Preacher looked down at himself. "I spect you're right." He sighed. "We ain't been sleepin' in beds lately."

Esek glanced around them. "Let's git us a drink first . . ." He walked into the saloon, a long, dark room that smelled of coal oil, beer, and tobacco. There was one man behind the long bar; he was in shirtsleeves with a red cravat, and his black hair was slicked back so it looked painted on. He served them beer, and Esek asked the name of the town.

"Fadden. You gents here for the drummers' meetin'?"

Esek was surprised when Preacher said, "Yeah. Where is the meet?"

"At the Haver House, down the block." The barman jerked his thumb.

"Thanks, brother."

Outside, Esek said, "What the hell you want goin' to a meetin' for?"

"Something might turn up." Preacher grinned and indicated a sign across the street. "Let's go get us a bath. Then we can buy them new duds."

The dry goods store clerk outfitted them in store suits

right off the rack. Preacher chose black as usual; Esek admired himself in a brown check with a new white shirt and celluloid collar. Their boots had been polished by a lad as they bathed. Esek thought they looked very stylish as they walked across to the hotel.

The Haver House had a large ballroom, which had been decorated with red, white, and blue bunting, white Chinese lanterns, and red paper bells. It looked very festive.

There were possibly twenty-five men milling about, talking and laughing, with several overdressed girls with trays serving drinks from the bar, set up at the end of the room. There were also a number of booths along one wall, displaying various goods. Esek had never seen so many salesmen at one place before in his life.

Preacher mingled, talking to various groups, but Esek went back to the hotel lobby and gathered up a stack of newspapers. He went through them, looking for items about him and Preacher, and found none. Apparently they were old news. He smiled; that was all to the good.

Preacher joined him later, insisting they go back down the street to the saloon to talk.

"Why can't we talk here?"

"I d'want nobody to remember us together."

In the saloon, seated at a table by the wall, Esek said, "What you want to talk about?"

"Money. We got us a little money now, but not enough to retire on."

"Retire? Izzat what you got in mind?"

"Lissen, we can't be runnin' from the damn law all our lives, can we? One of these days they going to get lucky. Then we'll be back in prison . . ."

"All right. You said something might turn up."

Preacher nodded. "I think we might make a killin' here."

"How? Rob one of them drummers?"

"No. Something else."

Esek was annoyed. Preacher liked to draw things out. He stared at the other man. "What?"

Preacher lowered his voice. "I seen one of them hotel clerks put money in the safe behind the desk. A lot of money."

Esek stared at him. "The hotel safe! Jesus, I never thought of that!"

"Folks who stay at the hotel puts money in it too. They might be a pile in there—enough for us to retire on."

"You got a plan?"

"I got enough to talk about. There's a stable behind the hotel where we can leave our horses. We can go west from there into the hills—"

"What about the safe?"

Preacher nodded. "I seen him put the money in, but he didn't lock it. They probably uses the safe all the time so it'd be a lot of trouble lockin' and unlockin' it all day long. Here's what I figger. We go in late, making sure the safe is unlocked—we give the clerk something to put in it. Then we tie him up and go out the back to the stable and into the hills. No shootin'. No noise. That way we might have a hour start—dependin' on how soon they finds him."

Esek grinned. "Hell, you got a good plan. I like that part about givin' him something to put in it."

"All them drummers stayin' at the hotel—we just mix in with 'em. The night clerk won't know all their names."

"Then we do it tonight?"

"Why not?" Preacher nodded. "We best git us a couple sacks to put the money in." He tapped the table. "But no shooting. We want to get away slick and quiet."

Esek agreed, thinking again of New Orleans. Maybe this was the ticket!

They lost the trail as it began to get dark. Deputy Harris called a halt, and they prepared to camp for the night. Jessie asked, "Where would two men be likely to go from here?"

Harris said, "You got your choice of three towns . . . if they going to a town, and I spect they would." He drew a map in the dirt. "This here's Haywood." He made a dot. "It's about forty mile due west." He poked another dot. "This here's Fadden. It's about half a day's ride south." He made another dot. "This's Grime's Creek. It's about thirty mile southeast." He looked at them. "Them three is the closest."

"Which is the largest?" Ki asked.

"Fadden, prob'ly."

"The bigger the town," Jessie said, "the easier to hide in, wouldn't you say?"

Harris nodded. "A stranger wouldn't stick out so much. You going to Fadden then?"

Ki glanced at Jessie, and smiled. "Reckon so."

Harris and the posse spent the next morning looking for the trail and finally gave it up and went home. Late that afternoon, Jessie and Ki rode into Fadden. There were two hotels. The largest was full up with a meeting of drummers, so they got rooms at the Traveler's, and Ki began to make his usual inquiries, though he expected no result. Preacher and Esek had money from the Dykes's robbery-murder.

No one had been delivering sermons in the saloons, he told Jessie over supper. "How's your hunch? Are they in this town?"

"My hunch is on vacation, I'm afraid. It's not telling me a thing."

A light rain fell that night and Jessie woke to find the streets muddy. It was still misting when she and Ki went to breakfast—and heard the news.

The Haver House had been robbed the night before.

Preacher had waited in the hallway while Esek tied both horses, bedrolls and food sacks fastened onto their saddles, in the large stable. The stableman, if there was one, was doubtless asleep somewhere.

They went together to the hotel desk, where a single clerk was dozing. It was after midnight, and the ballroom had been closed for more than an hour. The safe was locked.

Esek woke the clerk and handed him an envelope with a room number marked on it. "Put this in the safe, please."

The man yawned, took the envelope, and nodded sleepily.

Esek slid behind the desk, and when the man knelt down and opened the safe, Esek hit him sharply with the barrel of his revolver. The man collapsed with hardly a sound and lay, breathing shallowly.

They filled two sacks with greenbacks, coins, and jewelry, locked the safe again, and hurried out to the horses. They rode away in the misting rain, pointing west.

Luck was running their way, Esek said cheerfully. "I told you it was gonna change."

An hour after sunup they came to a well-rutted road and turned into it, heading north. It rained and misted all that day, and by nightfall they came to a little settlement—a few houses astride the road, a store, a stable, and a deadfall. They spent the night in the stable, deciding to head east on the stage. There was a stage station in Madison, the owner told them. It was a day's ride north.

The owner of the stable was a man named Fritz Yager, bulky, always unshaven, and friendless, even in a tiny burg of less than a hundred persons. He lived behind the stable in a smelly room, and when he saw the greenbacks in Preacher's hands, as he was paid for space and oats, he determined to have the wad.

He sat in his room, thinking about it. There must have been several hundred dollars in Preacher's hands. And maybe the other one, the stocky man, might have the same . . . or more. His stable was worth little—even if someone wanted to buy it, which was not likely. The money the two travelers had would enable him to go east again to New England. He rubbed his big hands together in anticipation.

He'd wait till they were asleep in the stalls, finish them off, tie the bodies onto the horses, and light out long before dawn. Then he'd dump the bodies miles from the settle-

144

ment, in the desert, and go on to Madison. It ought to be easy.

And no one would miss him . . . or the two travelers. Everyone would assume they'd all gone away together. Wouldn't they? Even if they thought something else, they would probably do nothing about it. The nearest law was a long way off.

But Fritz Yager was a stableman, not an owlhoot. He had never been on the shady side of the law for anything serious. He went about killing the two travelers in too clumsy a manner. When he opened the door to the stable, it squeaked, and candlelight streamed out.

He had five stalls, and he walked to the first, where the two pilgrims were sleeping, his shadow on the walls, huge and menacing.

He had a singletree that had been sawn in half as a club. As he lifted the club, Esek shot him three times at close range, slamming him down to sprawl in the dirt. Esek got up and bent over the body, poking it with the muzzle of his Colt.

He looked back at Preacher, "The son of a bitch was gonna whack us with this." He held up the heavy club.

Preacher stood up. "We best light out. No tellin' if he got friends . . ."

They saddled the horses, tied on the bedrolls, and opened the stable door. There was a light on in another building, and somene yelled, "What was that shootin'?"

Esek said to Preacher, "I got no idee." They mounted and loped along the road in the dark.

★
Chapter 23

Jessie and Ki went to the Haver House at once, only to learn that the night clerk had just died. He had been hit a hard blow on the head and had not regained consciousness.

The hotel owner opened the safe and discovered that it had been cleaned out.

No one had seen anything. There were no suspects.

Jessie said to Ki, "Preacher and Esek Kite, do you think?"

"Of course it's possible."

They talked to the town marshal later in his office, explaining that they had followed the two fugitives from Leavenworth.

The safe had contained about three thousand dollars in cash and jewels, the marshal told them. He was very interested in their opinion that it might have been Preacher and Esek—he had a flyer on them, and they became his best suspects.

But he had no idea where to start looking for the two.

Jessie said, "So far they've left a trail of murder, and it seems likely they'll go on doing more of the same."

Ki agreed. "Three thousand isn't enough to keep them for very long. And I have one other point . . ."

"What is it?"

"This is a sparsely settled land, with not too many opportunities for getting money the way they get it. How long will they stay here?"

"A very good point," Jessie said. "But which way will they go . . . back toward the east, or to California?"

"Or Mexico," Ki replied.

It was three days later that a rider brought the news that a stable owner had been shot to death in his own stable by two men passing through.

Ki talked to the rider in a saloon, asking where the shooting had taken place. Then he and Jessie went there at once—a weather-beaten cluster of buildings astride the trail. The victim, Fritz Yager, had already been buried. No one knew why he'd been shot.

The storekeeper told them, "Fritz was shot three times, prob'ly from about three feet away. They was two men staying overnight in the stable, but I don't know their names. They was gone by morning when we looked in the stable."

"You waited till morning?"

The storekeeper shrugged. "They mighta been crazy folks waitin' to shoot whoever held the lantern."

"Did you see either of the strangers?"

"I remember one. He was a tall gent, in black, kind of stooped when he walked."

"Preacher," Ki said.

Jesse persisted, "You've no idea why this Fritz Yager was shot?"

The storekeeper shook his head. "No idee at all." He scratched a stubbled chin. "But I got to say this. Fritz, he was a snarly sort. Didn't have many friends. Maybe he got into a argument with 'em."

When they left the store, Ki said, "An argument? What would they argue about?"

"Maybe Fritz overcharged them for sleeping in his stable."

"Money . . ." Ki mused. "Yes, it could be about money. What if Fritz saw they had money on them?"

"And he tried to rob them!"

"And got shot for his efforts. That's a better reason than an argument."

Jessie said, "And it's in keeping with their characters. They shot down an unarmed man in the cattle dealer's

147

office. I'm sure if Fritz made the slightest move they'd shoot him."

Ki nodded and looked at the sky. "Which way did they go? I vote for north."

"So do I. The nearest town's that way."

"And the rain has let up for the time being. Madison's a day's ride north. Maybe we can beat the rain there."

Madison was a town in a jumble of small hills. It had started as a mining camp, the hotel clerk told Preacher. Then it had grown in all directions with no one to organize it or tame it. The main street was at the bottom of a shallow canyon, winding idly along, with a few short cross streets. It was the county seat, with a courthouse and other county buildings around a small square park that had a civil war cannon in its center.

Esek went to the stage office and came back to the hotel. "Stage goes east in two days. Reckon we got to sit here."

Preacher shrugged. "Give us a chance to catch up on our sleep."

"When we git on that stage, where you want to get off?"

Preacher studied the other man. "Never give it a minute's thought. We don't want to go back to Leavenworth . . ."

"Hell no."

"What if we go down to Texas? I never been to Santone or Fort Worth . . ."

"What about one of them cow towns on the railroad? There's cow dealers in 'em. Abilene or one of them others."

Preacher nodded. "That's a idee. And this time we see if they's a herd in the pens."

The clerk, Isa Daws, was a man in his early twenties; his father was a deputy sheriff and the clerk had ideas of going into that trade. When he saw Preacher, and talked to him, it stirred his memory. He went to his father's office when he got off duty and asked to look through the wanted dodgers.

"What're you after?" his father asked.

"There's a man came into the hotel—I think I remember reading something that reminded me—yes, here it is. Chaney Hanks, known as 'Preacher.' Convicted of murder-robbery. One thousand dollars reward. Known to travel with Esek Kite, also wanted. Hanks is tall and slightly stooped, dark mustache, wears black as a rule. Is known to give sermons to pass the hat. He is armed and dangerous."

His father said, "And you think he's staying at the hotel?"

"I know he is. And the other one too, Kite."

"Don't you do a thing. Don't even look at them. Lemme talk to the sheriff. He's at the main office . . ." His father hurried out.

Instead of going home, Isa went back to the hotel. If there was going to be excitement, he wanted to see it. And figures danced in his head. One thousand dollars reward! It would be his when the two crooks were apprehended! What he could do with a thousand dollars! It boggled the mind.

Another clerk was on duty, Jonas Pike, a much older man who had a drinking problem. He usually got through an eight-hour stretch without becoming incoherent, but the ten-hour duty period often incapacitated him. However, the owner was never around that late, which had saved him so far.

Isa debated telling him of the two dangerous characters in the hotel, and finally concluded not to. Jonas really could not be trusted.

But Jonas was curious why he was there.

"I'm meeting somebody here later," Isa said, which in a way was close to the truth.

His father, Sheriff Blenker, and two other deputies showed up in an hour. Blenker wanted to know, "Are they in their rooms?"

"Yes," Isa said. "At least they didn't come down here."

His father said, "You better go home. There's liable to be shooting."

"I want to see what happens."

"Then stay here, behind the desk."

Blenker said, "Which rooms are they in?"

Isa looked at the cubby holes. "204 and 207."

"Is there only one way in and out?"

"Yes. Only one door to a room."

"Do the rooms have adjoining doors?"

"No. But there's the windows, one to a room."

"Could they jump out?"

Isa said, "I dunno about them, but I could. It's not that far down."

"Damn," the sheriff said. "Tim, you 'n' Frank get around the side there in case they come out the window." He looked at Isa. "You said 204 and 207? Are they on opposite sides of the hall?"

"Yes, they are. But the 207 side is close to another building and it's dark as hell when you look down at this time of night. They might not want to jump out, not knowing what they'd land on."

"All right, then you boys go around to—which side?"

Isa pointed. "The left side."

The two deputies nodded and hurried out.

Sheriff Blenker pulled his Colt, drew back the hammer, and turned the cylinder, looking at the brass. "You ready, Ben?"

"Yeah . . . let's go."

They went up the stairs. At the top Blenker said, "They both might be in the same room. We'll rap on the door and when they open it, we'll go in quick. All right?"

Ben Daws nodded.

They walked down the hall to 204. Blenker looked at Ben, raised his fist, and rapped several times. There was no answer, no sound from inside the room.

Esek had gone out to a store and brought back bread, cheese, and sliced meat to Preacher's hotel room, 207. He spread it out on the bed and they ate in silence. Esek had seen a poster, he said, describing them and offering

150

a thousand dollar reward. The description was mostly of Preacher, and in the morning he would go out and buy a linen duster for Preacher to wear, concealing his black clothes when they got on the stage.

When they finished eating, Preacher rolled up the remaining bread and cheese for breakfast. Esek went to the door, opened it, and closed it at once.

"There's men in the hall at my door."

Preacher jumped up. "How many?"

"Two."

Esek opened the door a crack. "They're going in the room—come on—it's our chance t'go down the back stairs!"

They hurried out and along the hall. As they reached the stairs, a shot slammed into the wall over their heads and someone yelled.

Esek turned and fired four times, as fast as he could thumb the hammer, then he followed Preacher. They went out the back door into the dark. There was no time to saddle the horses. Preacher turned right along the alley, running awkwardly, swearing under his breath.

At the first break in the alley, he turned left, ran between two shacks, and gained the next street. They could hear men shouting behind them. Preacher stopped, panting hard, gasping for breath. But Esek propelled him along. "We got to keep moving."

At the end of the block, they turned back toward the main street, and before them was a long hitch rack with half a dozen saddled horses waiting. Esek smiled.

Preacher said, "The Lord will provide!"

They selected two horses and swung up.

Preacher and Esek had been in Madison, so Sheriff Blenker told Jessie and Ki, but they had escaped.

"It was night and we couldn't tell which way they went," Blenker said, as they sat in his office. "We know they stole two horses and they left ever'thing behind—bedrolls

151

and what vittles they had. They got away with what they had on."

"It's lucky no one was hurt." Jessie said. "Those two are killers."

"One of 'em fired four times at us in the hall, but we ducked into the room . . . You say you follered them from Leavenworth?"

"Yes. This is about the closest we've come. We suspect they came here to take the stage," Jessie said. "We don't know which way."

"I expect you've been at the telegraph . . . ," Ki said.

"Yes, for an hour or more."

"Then there's not much more we can do but wait," Jessie said. "They'll have to surface soon for food, if nothing else."

Esek led them east from Madison, following a rutted wagon track that veered from the stage road, pointing more east and south. They might be expected to follow the road, Esek said.

When they halted after an hour to breathe the horses, Preacher said, "How'd they know it was us in that hotel?"

"Prob'ly a flyer. They got descriptions of us. Somebody seen us and wants the reward. We got to lay low until folks forgets about us."

"You got an idee how we can do that?"

"No." Esek shook his head. "But we got to do it." He looked at Preacher critically. "One thing we could do—"

"What?"

"Split up. You go one way and me the other. They lookin' for two of us together."

Preacher looked up at the dark sky and sighed. "You figger that would gain us much?"

"Maybe not. Hard to tell. You want to think about it?"

"No, I reckon not. Things is all right the way they is."

Esek nodded. "Then let's make tracks."

152

The wagon track joined with another, and shortly after sunup, it turned south after skirting a group of low sand hills.

Esek pulled up. "You want to go south? There ain't nothing thataway except 'dobe shacks, rattlesnakes, and buzzards."

"We need vittles. That road might lead us to some."

"And it might not. I vote we go on east."

Preacher shaded his eyes and peered toward the south, seeing only rolling prairie. He let his breath out and nodded. "All right. Let's go east."

★
Chapter 24

They came to the broad trail at midday. It came from the north and wandered off to the south and east, where there was a haze of smoke on the horizon.

They followed the trail for an hour, and then, on a rise, Preacher examined the smoke with the binoculars and declared it came from a chimney.

He was proved right. The smoke was only a wisp when they got close. It came from one of the two chimneys of a trading post, a very solid-looking building of logs and mud that squatted by the trail, facing a narrow brown stream. Beyond the post alongside the creek were three tepees, where a few brown-skinned children splashed and yelled.

The trading post's owner was Lucas Quitman; his name was painted above the door. He was a big, quick-eyed man, dark as any Indian, with a toothy smile that did not reach his eyes. He demanded news and they told him what they could.

Preacher asked, "Them Sioux, by the creek there?"

"No. Arapahoes. Where you gents headin'?"

"South," Esek said. "Figger to go down to Texas."

"That's a mighty sizeable place, Texas . . ."

"San Antone," Preacher said, glancing at Esek. "We got kin there."

Lucas nodded. "I was there ten, twelve year ago. How you happen to come this way?"

"Dumb luck, brother, just dumb luck."

"Is they a posse on your tail?"

Esek growled. He opened his coat and rested one hand

on the revolver butt. "That make a difference t'you?"

Lucas smiled. "Just gabbin', gents. No offense intended." He spoke over his shoulder. "Easy, Maja."

They looked to see an Indian woman with a double-barreled shotgun, which was resting on some grain sacks and pointed at their middles.

Preacher said, "Peace, brother. We come to buy us some vittles."

Lucas stood in the doorway, smoking his pipe, watching the two strangers make camp in a grove of trees several hundred yards from the store, in the opposite direction from the tepees. They made a fire and went about fixing themselves supper. Lucas waited patiently as they settled down, then he went back into the store and found his son eating supper at the table. The boy was seventeen, as tall as his father but thin and wiry.

Lucas said, "You git on your pony and take this here paper to the law in Madison."

"What is it?"

"It's a wanted dodger." He laid it on the table and tapped it. "You tell the law that them two is camped here by the crick."

The boy read the poster that had been brought by a traveler a week past. "A thousand dollars!"

"That's right. We git it if them two is caught. You walk that horse away nice and easy so they don't hear you, then you ride like hell, hear?"

The lad grinned, shoved the paper into a pocket, and hurried out.

It was dark, the fire very low, when Preacher said, "Saddle them horses, Esek. It don't feel right here."

"Them Indians is Arapahoes."

"It ain't the Indians. I got an itchy feelin' about that Lucas feller. He got a shifty look to him."

"What can he do?"

"I dunno what the hell he can do, but it don't feel easy. Besides he sure asks a lot of questions."

"You want to relocate?"

"Let's wait an hour or two. Let 'em think we're sleeping."

Esek dumped dirt on the fire, and they saddled the horses, then rolled the blankets and tied them on. Esek led the way upstream when the hour had passed. The trading post was closed and silent.

A half mile upstream they mounted and turned eastward.

Esek said, "How you feel now?"

Preacher grunted. "Don't josh me, Esek, dammit! Somethin' was wrong back there. I dunno what it was, but it was there."

"That post is fifty miles from nowhere. You just got a itch in your butt."

"Maybe so. But anyways, it's gone now."

The boy, Alden Quitman, delivered his message to Sheriff Wilfred Blenker. He laid the poster on the desk. "My pa says these two men is at the post, camped by the crick."

Blenker sat up quickly. "They're there now? You saw 'em yourself?"

"Sure I did."

"When did you see 'em last?"

"Just before I left, last night after dark."

Blenker organized a posse at once, including Jessie and Ki. They rode out minutes after noon, with the boy as guide. The trading post, a dot in the vastness, would be easy to miss. But the lad had made the trip to Madison dozens of times from the age of five.

Blenker said to the lad, "We'll stop a mile from the post and you go in on foot so nobody sees you. Can you do that?"

"Of course."

"All right. Find out where them two are, and come back."

"They camped by the crick."

156

"I got to know exactly. Maybe they moved."

The boy shrugged and slid off the pony.

He was back in half an hour. "They both gone, Sheriff. Pa says they wasn't there this morning."

Blenker swore.

He had said nothing to the fugitives, Quitman told the sheriff. They had certainly not detected the boy leaving. "It must be they just got the wind up, Sheriff."

Blenker nodded sadly. Who could outguess an owlhoot? They didn't know themselves what they would do next. He had his men spread out and look for tracks, but there were too many, and he gave it up and headed back to Madison.

Jessie and Ki, however, decided to go on east, convinced the two were pointed that way, despite what Quitman told them about Texas. If Preacher and Esek said they were going to Texas, then it was probably the last place to look for them.

According to their map, the stage road from Madison ran generally east for a hundred or more miles through wild country. There were lonely little way stations and a few towns along the route, but nothing else.

Ki said, "It seems to me they'd follow the stage road if they could. Moving across country would be slower, and dangerous. Any band of hostiles would attack two whites alone . . ."

"I agree. Let's take the road ourselves. Maybe we'll get lucky."

They followed the road to Enders, a town the size of Madison. It was built near an army fort of the same name and was a windy, dusty place with only one redeeming feature. The sun went down at night.

Ki made the rounds of the seven saloons, and as far as he could learn, Preacher and Esek had not been there. If they had come to town, they had not made one single ripple. Nothing like the ripples Jessie made as she rode in.

A crowd gathered each time she showed herself. The hotel clerk told Ki the town had not seen a real woman for a year. "Only them whores at the saloon. Well, there's a couple wives in town, but they don't count. They old anyhow."

The town marshal had not seen Preacher and Esek either, and he had a flyer on the two. "I'm keepin' my eyes open," he told them. "I could use that thousand dollars they offering for Hanks."

The hotel was next to the stageline yard; they decided to wait a few days. As Ki said, they could give a good look at each passenger who got off the coaches.

"Even if Preacher tries to disguise himself, I think we'd recognize him."

The town was not on a telegraph line; the only wire in the territory followed the railroad, much farther north.

Their third day in the town was unproductive. Jessie was feeling restive. "I'm afraid we've missed them."

Ki was inclined to agree. "Maybe we'd better go on eastward. They could be putting more and more distance between us."

"Yes." It was frustrating doing nothing. "When d'you want to go?"

"Why not first thing in the morning?"

"All right."

And then that afternoon late, a rider came into town, covered with dust. He was young, maybe nineteen, and had just ridden from Buckey, a town some thirty miles south. Ki heard him talking in a saloon. Someone had gunned down the town deputy.

"I seen the whole thing," the young man said. "This feller was standin' at the bar when the deputy come in. The deputy says something to him . . . and the feller turns and shoots—not a word, just shoots—just like that. Three shots. Then him and another feller walks out."

Ki asked, "What did the shooter look like?"

"Tall, sort of stooped gent."

"How was he dressed?"

"Black store clothes."

158

Ki smiled. "Thanks."

"It has to be Preacher," he said to Jessie in the hotel. "There can't be another like him in the area. He was with a second man, who must be Esek."

"Then we go to Buckey," she said.

There was a trail of sorts. Apparently not many made that trip. They saw no one and arrived in Buckey just after midday to hear that a group of men had gone after the two who had shot the deputy.

"They wasn't no law with 'em," a bartender told Ki. "He was the only law we had . . . and well thought of. Folks hated to hear about him bein' shot down thataway."

A number of porch sitters had seen the five men ride out after the two killers. "They went east, miss," a man told Jessie, jerking his thumb. "You be lucky to catch 'em now."

Preacher and Esek got into Buckey late in the afternoon. They got down in front of the Three Barrels Saloon, and Preacher said he was thirsty.

Esek said, "We oughta get us a place to stay the night."

"Right after we gets us a drink." Preacher led the way into the saloon, paying no attention to a drifter in ragged clothes who stared at him and took several steps after him, then turned and hurried away across the dusty street.

Preacher ordered beer at the bar and looked around the room as he gulped it. Esek sipped his and fished for a stub of cigar. He frowned at the solidly built man who stepped inside the door of the saloon and looked hard at each man at the bar. He had started to nudge Preacher when the man approached and said, "You're Preacher Hanks—"

Preacher turned, drawing his revolver—and fired three times.

As the man dropped, sprawling on the hard floor, Preacher glanced around the room. Then he and Esek walked out, got on the horses, and rode away.

★

Chapter 25

Dusk was not far off when they left the town behind. They followed no road, which was a good thing, Preacher said. "They can't track us over the grass."

"It ain't all grass." Esek growled. He was unhappy about the shooting. It put them on the run again, just when he'd been thinking about a real bed.

On the first rise they halted and listened, hearing no sounds of pursuit. "He was a lawman," Preacher said. "I seen the star on his belt. They must got posters out ever'where for us."

"Yeah. So why don't we go over to Missouri? They's places there that nobody will ever think of looking for us."

Preacher lifted a bushy eyebrow. "You want to hide all your life?"

"I want to stay alive!" Esek made a face. "Hell, they got enough on us now to hang us forty times over."

"If they catch us. If. We got to get off'n this damn prairie into a big town—maybe Kansas City."

"Or New Orleans."

"Yeah, that's right. They play hell catchin' us in a big town, long's we don't pull nothing there. We'd make a few changes—but one thing though—"

"What?"

"Money. We need more money. We ain't got enough between us t'lie up for a year till all the fuss dies down."

Esek nodded, agreeing. They needed four or five thousand rock bottom to feel comfortable. There was no telling what expenses might be necessary to a man on the run.

160

"We git off'n the high plains," Preacher said, "we start lookin' at banks."

They kept going through the night, navigating by the stars, keeping as much as possible to a straight line. Even a slight deviation a few degrees by their pursuers would put them miles off to the right or left.

In the morning they could see no one on their trail. Preacher used the binoculars on every higher rise of ground, shaking his head each time—until he spotted the tepees.

"Indians out there to the right," he said. "Could be Sioux." They veered to the left.

Esek said, "Wonder how Runnin' Wolf is these days . . ."

"We best not run into him. He never did git those Henry rifles. He likely harborin' a grudge."

Esek chuckled. That was the God's truth . . .

They came to Frypan two days later.

It was a town built in a little valley among lodgepole pines; it straggled along a creek not far from the desert, and though it had obviously been there a long time, it did not appear on their map.

The single main street was quiet in midday, a few horses standing three-footed at hitch racks, but no wagons. A few people were on the street to stare at them. The two saloons they passed were open. They got down in front of the hotel, a seedy-looking two-story building with the word "Hotel" in flaking white paint over the door.

Preacher said, leaning on the horse, "Never seed such a quiet town."

"Maybe everybody's asleep."

Inside the building, three steps up from the boardwalk, the desk room was tiny, hardly room enough for a counter and chair behind it. An older man with glasses halfway down his nose frowned at them from behind the counter and put down a newspaper. "You all just come in?"

Esek said, "What's the name of this place anyway?"

"Frypan. You stayin' the night? Four bits each." He

161

jerked his thumb toward the narrow stairs. "Any room you wants, gents."

"You got a stable?"

"Next door." He inclined his head. "Privy's out back." He took a dollar from Preacher and put it in his pocket.

Jessie and Ki rode east from Buckey for two days and halted in Alders, a shabby town built close to a spring and pond. It took only a short while to be certain Preacher and Esek had not been there.

After talking to bartenders, Ki said, "I doubt if they came along this way at all."

Jessie asked, "What's south of here?"

"Desert, a few mountains, lots of jackrabbits and cactus."

"No towns at all?"

Ki spread out their map. "A few, yes. Here, here, and here. But not much, I'm afraid." He moved his finger to the south. "I'm told that from this place south there's no law at all—all the way to Mexico."

Jessie sighed. "It sounds like the area where Preacher and Esek would thrive."

"Yes, it does."

They slept in beds that night and turned their horses' heads south in the morning.

Days later, long after dark, they came into Frypan. Only one saloon was open, and the clerk in the only hotel was asleep in his chair.

Ki smiled at Jessie. "Shall we wake him up or let him sleep?"

"Let him sleep. We can pay him in the morning."

Ki put their horses in the stable, and Jessie carried the bedrolls to the rooms. Most of the room doors were standing open. She selected two and dropped the bedding on the cots.

Preacher went downstairs in the morning and asked the sleepy-eyed clerk, "Anybody come in last night?"

"No. Nobody."

Preacher nodded, and Esek said, "Is there any law in town?"

"Law in Frypan!?" The clerk laughed. "Hell no. They was a posse come in two, three year ago, but folks run 'em out."

"Who runs the town then?"

"Some of the merchants does. Like Turk, who owns this here hotel and some of the saloons. You don't cross them."

"Peace, brother. We's peaceable pilgrims."

They went across the street to Rose's Restaurant, and Esek said, "This here's an outlaw town. If we stay here, they going to send us a bill."

"You think so?"

"Sure. Gents comes here to lay up from the law. They got to split with the town."

"Then we best git us some vittles and slide out."

Esek nodded and pushed his coffee cup away. "I'll get the horses. Meet you at the store."

Jessica wore boots, jeans, a denim coat, and a black ribbon in her glossy hair when she went downstairs in the morning.

The clerk was astounded, staring at her. His mouth dropped open. "Where'd you come from?"

"You were asleep when we came in last night, so we didn't wake you."

Ki came down behind her and gave the clerk money as she went to the street door. She opened it and paused. "Ki!"

Preacher was crossing the street toward them!

As she spoke, he looked up and saw her. Instantly he halted, pulled a pistol, and fired, all in one quick motion. The bullet smashed the lintel over her head. A second bullet went wild. Preacher began to run to the left, yelling to someone.

163

Jessie ran out to the walk and lifted her Colt, but Preacher was in among the horses and a bullet snapped over her head. She heard Ki shout to her, and she hurried back into the hotel.

In the next moment Preacher and Esek galloped away from the hitch rack, down the street, scattering a few early risers.

"The horses!" Ki yelled, and they ran for the stable.

It took minutes to saddle and bridle the horses, tie on the bedrolls, and gallop out to the street. Preacher and Esek had disappeared.

They galloped to the end of town and found that the road petered out. They could see no fresh tracks on the ground.

Jessie said, "They've been heading east. Let's go that way."

They put spurs to the horses, hurrying out onto the grass—and found nothing. Miles to the east, they saw no riders at all and could discover no evidence of anyone having passed that way recently.

Ki halted and stared back the way they'd come. "I think we've been suckered . . . What if they made a circle and went back to the town?"

"And let us wander around out here . . ."

"Chasing our tails. Yes."

She said, "If they did go back, they've probably told everyone that we're the law."

Ki frowned. "That's not good. The clerk told us that a posse was run out. We'd better wait until dark before going back."

★

Chapter 26

Preacher had been astonished to see the girl—he knew who she was instantly—at the door of the hotel. He and Esek had tried to kill her companion, the Chinaman, a long time ago, and had hit someone else instead. He drew his pistol and fired at her, then ran for Esek and the horses. Did she have a posse with her?

Esek was startled to hear the shot. He saw the girl too and fired too hastily, swearing. Preacher shouted at him to mount, they had to get out of town. He flung himself onto the horse and dug in the spurs. He yelled, "How'd she find us here?"

Preacher didn't answer. He glanced behind them—no one was coming after. He swerved and rode between buildings and gained the open fields with Esek pounding along behind.

A mile from the town, Preacher reined in under a copse of trees and looked back. "We ain't got a single can of beans! Let's circle around. Maybe we can lose 'em!"

Esek stood in the stirrups, peering at the distant town. There was no pursuit so far. "All right . . ." He followed Preacher's lead.

They galloped north till the rooflines were out of sight, then turned west. When they approached the town again it was from the southwest. They got down behind the livery and led the horses past the corrals.

The owner saw them and came out of the shade, pushing up his hat. "Didn't I seen you fellers jest ride out of town?"

"Pinkertons after us, brother," Preacher said. "We had t'skedaddle."

"Pinkertons! Jesus! That's the first they been here in five year!"

"Mighty pushy folks."

The liveryman peered westward. "You figger you lost 'em?"

"Hope so. But if they comes in here, you ain't seen us."

"My eyes going bad," the man agreed. "Can't see a foot in front of me."

They left the horses in the stable and went into the saloon next door. As soon as it got dark, Preacher said, they would make themselves scarce.

Long after dark they entered the town again quietly, walking the horses. The saloons were all open; light was streaming into the shadowy street, and music was playing.

If Preacher and Esek were in the town, how would they get them out? There was no law to help. The nearest lawman was in Madison; he might as well be on the moon.

It was a problem they would face—when they faced it, Ki said.

They took rooms in the hotel again, and this time the clerk was awake. His eyes rounded on seeing Jessica once more. "I thought you two rode out!"

Ki smiled. "We rode back."

"You ain't going to shoot us up again are you?"

Ki reminded him, "Somebody else was shooting at *us.*"

The clerk was stubborn. "Well my boss don't like bullet holes in the hotel." But he took their money.

When they were alone, Ki said, "Better holes in the hotel than in us."

They dropped the bedrolls in adjoining rooms and went out to the street to look for Preacher and Esek. The two might be in the town—and they might be halfway to Kansas City.

They were, in fact, in the Senate Saloon, sitting at a side table. Esek had a deck of cards and was playing solitaire while Preacher smoked a cigar and watched. The saloon was crowded and smoky, but Preacher noticed them at once when the Chinaman and the girl entered. They stood by the door looking at the room.

Preacher hissed at Esek and grabbed his arm. "Them two—they're here!"

"Where?" Esek swung around, staring.

"Over by the door."

"Son of a bitch!" Esek slid his gun out.

Preacher grabbed at him. "Don't go shooting no woman! They'll string us up!"

Esek growled and jerked his arm away. "Izzit all right for her to shoot at us?"

Preacher let out his breath. "Let's slide out easy. Go to the back . . ."

Esek got up. "The girl—she went out the door."

"Let 'er go . . . Come on."

They shoved their way through the crowds gathered about the tables and were separated in a moment. And suddenly, at the end of the long bar, Esek came face-to-face with the Chinaman, who smiled at him. They were some fifteen feet apart, and Esek glanced around for Preacher and did not see him. But he saw that the Chinaman did not wear a gun, and Esek's face crinkled into a grin. Too bad, you damn Chinee . . .

His hand went for the Colt, drew it—and instantly there was a flash of silver in the air. Esek fired into the floor. He heard the shot—but nothing else—

Ki knelt by the downed man and retrieved the *shuriken,* wiping it on Esek's shirt. Esek had seen he wore no pistol, and would have shot him down. But he had been slower than the throwing star that had torn out his throat.

167

The crowd pressed around, curious: "How'd he git dead?" and "What happened?" They stared at the body and at Ki. Someone said they ought to call the doc.

Ki rose and made his way through them to the back door. Preacher must have gone out to the alley . . . But he saw no one. It was very dark, however, and a man could hide in a hundred places. Ki hurried around to the front of the saloon. Jessie was there, by the horses.

"Neither of them came out here . . ." She looked at him anxiously. "What was that shot?"

He explained quickly. "Preacher got away—he must be somewhere in the town."

She frowned at the dark street. "We'll never find him tonight . . ."

Preacher ran along the alley, dodged between buildings, and found a horse at a hitch rack. He climbed aboard and, keeping to the shadows, walked the animal out of town, toward the north. He and Esek had agreed that if they got separated by some circumstance they would meet again in Madison. From there they would take the stage east.

He had no food with him, not even a bedroll. But the town was only a few days away. He could put up with it, and the horse he'd stolen was a good, sound animal. He would keep going, sleep in the saddle . . .

The next afternoon late, he was walking the horse, dozing, when he heard the yips. He came awake, staring about him; the prairie seemed empty. And then suddenly they were all around him: mounted Sioux—with Running Wolf grinning at him!

They were well along the trail to Madison when they saw the buzzards circling in the cold blue sky. They headed that way and found the badly mutilated body in a shallow ravine.

Ki jumped down and made a quick examination, then

looked up at Jessie. "It's Preacher—or was—"

"Indians," she said.

"I'm afraid so. He's been scalped . . ."

She sighed. "He really didn't deserve much better . . ."

Watch for

LONE STAR AND THE BUCCANEERS

122nd novel in the exciting LONE STAR series
from Jove

Coming in October!

SPECIAL PREVIEW!

Award-winning author Bill Gulick presents his epic trilogy of the American West, the magnificent story of two brothers, Indian and white man, bound by blood and divided by destiny . . .

Northwest Destiny

This classic saga includes *Distant Trails, Gathering Storm,* and *River's End.*

Here is a special excerpt from Volume One, DISTANT TRAILS—available from Jove books . . .

For the last hundred yards of the stalk, neither man had spoken—not even in whispers—but communicated by signs as they always did when hunting meat to fill hungry bellies. Two steps ahead, George Drewyer, the man recognized to be the best hunter in the Lewis and Clark party, sank down on his right knee, froze, and peered intently through the glistening wet bushes and dangling evergreen tree limbs toward the animal grazing in the clearing. Identifying it, he turned, using his hands swiftly and graphically to tell the younger, less experienced hunter, Matt Crane, the nature of the animal he had seen and how he meant to approach and kill it.

Not a deer, his hands said. Not an elk. Just a stray Indian horse—with no Indians in sight. He'd move up on it from downwind, his hands said, until he got into sure-kill range, then he'd put a ball from his long rifle into its head. What he expected Matt to do was follow a couple of steps behind and a few feet off to the right, stopping when he stopped, aiming when he aimed, but firing only if the actions of the horse clearly showed that Drewyer's ball had missed.

Matt signed that he understood. Turning back toward the clearing, George Drewyer began his final stalk.

Underfoot, the leaf mold and fallen pine needles formed a yielding carpet beneath the scattered clumps of bushes and thick stands of pines, which here on the western slope of the Bitter Root Mountains were broader in girth and taller than the skinny lodgepole and larch found on the higher reaches of the Lolo Trail. Half a day's travel behind, the other thirty-two members of the party still were struggling in foot-deep snow over slick rocks, steep slides, and tangles of down timber treacherous as logjams, as they sought the headwaters of the Columbia and the final segment of their journey to the Pacific Ocean.

It had been four days since the men had eaten meat, Matt knew, being forced to sustain themselves on the detested army ration called "portable soup," a grayish brown jelly that looked like a mixture of pulverized wood duff and dried dung, tasted like iron filings, and even when flavored with meat drippings and dissolved in hot water satisfied the belly no more than a swallow of air. Nor had the last solid food been much, for the foal butchered at Colt-Killed Creek had been dropped by its dam only a few months ago; though its meat was tender enough, most of its growth had gone into muscle and bone, its immature carcass making skimpy portions when distributed among such a large party of famished men.

With September only half gone, winter had already come to the seven-thousand-foot-high backbone of the continent a week's travel behind. All the game that the old Shoshone guide, Toby, had told them usually was to be found in the high meadows at this time of year had moved down to lower levels. Desperate for food, Captain William Clark had sent George Drewyer and Matt Crane scouting ahead for meat, judging that two men traveling afoot and unencumbered would stand a much better chance of finding game than the main party with its thirty-odd men and twenty-nine heavily laden horses. As he usually did, Drewyer had found game of a sort, weighed the risk of rousing the hostility of its Indian owner against the need of the party for food, and decided that hunger recognized no property rights.

In the drizzling cold rain, the coat of the grazing horse glistened like polished metal. It would be around four years old, Matt guessed, a brown and white paint, well muscled, sleek, alert. If this were a typical Nez Perce horse, he could well believe what the Shoshone chief, Cameahwait, had told

Captain Clark—that the finest horses to be found in this part of the country were those raised by the Shoshones' mortal enemies, the Nez Perces. Viewing such a handsome animal cropping bluegrass on a Missouri hillside eighteen months ago, Matt Crane would have itched to rope, saddle, and ride it, testing its speed, wind, and spirit. Now all he itched to do was kill and eat it.

Twenty paces away from the horse, which still was grazing placidly, George Drewyer stopped, knelt behind a fallen tree, soundlessly rested the barrel of his long rifle on its trunk, and took careful aim. Two steps to his right, Matt Crane did the same. After what seemed an agonizingly long period of time, during which Matt held his breath, Drewyer's rifle barked. Without movement or sound, the paint horse sank to the ground, dead—Matt was sure—before its body touched the sodden earth.

"Watch it!" Drewyer murmured, swiftly reversing his rifle, swabbing out its barrel with the ramrod, expertly reloading it with patched and greased lead ball, wiping flint and firing hammer clean, then opening the pan and pouring in a carefully measured charge while he protected it from the drizzle with the tree trunk and his body.

Keeping his own rifle sighted on the fallen horse, Matt held his position without moving or speaking, as George Drewyer had taught him to do, until the swarthy, dark-eyed hunter had reloaded his weapon and risen to one knee. Peering first at the still animal, then moving his searching gaze around the clearing, Drewyer tested the immediate environment with all his senses—sight, sound, smell, and his innate hunter's instinct—for a full minute before he at last nodded in satisfaction.

"A bunch-quitter, likely. Least there's no herd nor herders around. Think you can skin it, preacher boy?"

"Sure. You want it quartered, with the innards saved in the hide?"

"Just like we'd do with an elk. Save everything but the hoofs and whinny. Get at it, while I snoop around for Injun sign. The Nez Perces will be friendly, the captains say, but I'd as soon not meet the Injun that owned that horse till its head and hide are out of sight."

While George Drewyer circled the clearing and prowled through the timber beyond, Matt Crane went to the dead horse, unsheathed his butcher knife, skillfully made the cuts needed to strip off the hide, and gutted and dissected the animal. Returning from his scout, Drewyer hunkered down beside him, quickly boned out as large a packet of choice cuts as he could conveniently carry, wrapped them in a piece of hide, and loaded the still-warm meat into the empty canvas backpack he had brought along for that purpose.

"It ain't likely the men'll get this far by dark," he said, "so I'll take 'em a taste to ease their bellies for the night. Can you make out alone till tomorrow noon?"

"Yes."

"From what I seen, the timber thins out a mile or so ahead. Seems to be a kind of open, marshy prairie beyond, which is where the Nez Perces come this time of year to dig roots, Toby says. Drag the head and hide back in the bushes out of sight. Cut the meat up into pieces you can spit and broil, then build a fire and start it cooking. If the smoke and smell brings Injun company, give 'em the peace sign, invite 'em to sit and eat, and tell 'em a big party of white men will be coming down the trail tomorrow. You got all that, preacher boy?"

"Yes."

"Good. Give me a hand with this pack and I'll be on my way." Slipping his arms through the straps and securing the pad that transferred a portion of the weight to his forehead, Drewyer got to his feet while Matt Crane eased the load. Grinning, Drewyer squeezed his shoulder. "Remind me to quit calling you preacher boy, will you, Matt? You've learned a lot since you left home."

"I've had a good teacher."

"That you have! Take care."

178

Left alone in the whispering silence of the forest and the cold, mist-like rain, Matt Crane dragged the severed head and hide into a clump of nearby bushes. Taking his hatchet, he searched for and found enough resinous wood, bark, and dry duff to catch the spark from his flint and steel. As the fire grew in the narrow trench he had dug for it, he cut forked sticks, placed pieces of green aspen limbs horizontally across them, sliced the meat into strips, and started it to broiling. The smell of juice dripping into the fire made his belly churn with hunger, tempting him to do what Touissant Charbonneau, the party's French-Canadian interpreter, did when fresh-killed game was brought into camp—seize a hunk and gobble it down hot, raw, and bloody. But he did not, preferring to endure the piercing hunger pangs just a little longer in exchange for the greater pleasure of savoring his first bite of well-cooked meat.

Cutting more wood for the fire, he hoped George Drewyer would stop calling him "preacher boy." Since at twenty he was one of the youngest members of the party and his father, the Reverend Peter Crane, was a Presbyterian minister in St. Louis, it had been natural enough for the older men to call him "the preacher's boy" at first. Among a less disciplined band, he would have been forced to endure a good deal of hoorawing and would have been the butt of many practical jokes. But the no-nonsense military leadership of the two captains put strict limits on that sort of thing.

Why Drewyer—who'd been raised a Catholic, could barely read and write, and had no peer as an outdoorsman—should have made Matt his protégé, Matt himself could not guess. Maybe because he was malleable, did what he was told to do, and never backed off from hard work. Maybe because he listened more than he talked. Or maybe because he was having the adventure of his life and showed it. Whatever the reason, their relationship was good. It would be even better, Matt mused, if Drewyer would drop the "preacher boy" thing and simply call him by name.

179

While butchering the horse, Matt noticed that it had been gelded as a colt. According to George Drewyer, the Nez Perces were one of the few Western Indian tribes that practiced selective breeding, thus the high quality of their horses. From the way Chief Cameahwait had acted, a state of war existed between the Shoshones and the Nez Perces, so the first contact between the Lewis and Clark party—which had passed through Shoshone country—and the Nez Perces was going to be fraught with danger. Aware of the fact that he might make the first contact, Matt Crane felt both uneasy and proud. Leaving him alone in this area showed the confidence Drewyer had in him. But his aloneness made him feel a little spooky.

With the afternoon only half gone and nothing to do but tend the fire, Matt stashed his blanket roll under a tree out of the wet, picked up his rifle, and curiously studied the surrounding forest. There was no discernible wind, but vagrant currents of air stirred, bringing to his nostrils the smell of wood smoke, of crushed pine needles, of damp leaf mold, of burnt black powder. As he moved across the clearing toward a three-foot-wide stream gurgling down the slope, he scowled, suddenly realizing that the burnt black powder smell could not have lingered behind this long. Nor would it have gotten stronger, as this smell was doing the nearer he came to the stream. Now he identified it beyond question.

Sulfur! There must be a mineral-impregnated hot spring nearby, similar to the hot springs near Traveler's Rest at the eastern foot of Lolo Pass, where the cold, weary members of the party had eased their aches and pains in warm, soothing pools. What he wouldn't give for a hot bath right now!

At the edge of the stream, he knelt, dipping his hand into the water. It was warm. Cupping his palm, he tasted it, finding it strongly sulfurous. If this were like the stream on the other side of the mountains, he mused, there would be one or more scalding, heavily impregnated springs issuing from old volcanic rocks higher up the slope, their waters diluted by colder side rivulets joining the main stream, making it simply a matter of exploration to find water temperature and a chemical content best suited to the needs of a cold, tired body. The prospect intrigued him.

Visually checking the meat broiling over the fire, he judged it could do without tending for an hour or so. Thick though the forest cover was along the sides of the stream, he would run no risk of getting lost, for following the stream downhill would bring him back to the clearing. Time enough then to cut limbs for a lean-to and rig a shelter for the night.

Sometimes wading in the increasingly warm waters of the stream, sometimes on its bush-bordered bank, he followed its windings uphill for half a mile before he found what he was looking for: a pool ten feet long and half as wide, eroded in smooth basalt, ranging in depth from one to four feet. Testing the temperature of its water, he found it just right—hot but not unbearably so, the sulfur smell strong but not unpleasant. Leaning his rifle against a tree trunk, he took off his limp, shapeless red felt hat, pulled his thin moccasins off his bruised and swollen feet, waded into the pool, and gasped with sensual pleasure as the heat of the water spread upward.

Since his fringed buckskin jacket and woolen trousers already were soaking wet from the cold rain, he kept them on as he first sank to a sitting position, then stretched out full length on his back, with only his head above water. After a time, he roused himself long enough to strip the jacket off over his head and pull the trousers down over his ankles. Tossing them into a clump of bushes near his rifle, hat, and moccasins, he lay back in the soothing water, naked, warm, and comfortable for the first time since Traveler's Rest.

Drowsily, his eyes closed. He slept . . .

The sound that awakened him some time later could have been made by a deer moving down to drink from the pool just upstream from where he lay. It could have been made by a beaver searching for a choice willow sapling to cut down. It could have been made by a bobcat, a bear, or a cougar. But as consciousness returned to him, as he heard the sound and attempted to identify it, his intelligence rejected each possibility that occurred to him the moment it crossed his mind—for one lucid reason.

Animals did not sing. And whatever this intruder into his state of tranquility might be, it was singing.

Though the words were not recognizable, they had an Indian sound, unmistakably conveying the message that the singer was at peace with the world, not self-conscious, and about to indulge in a very enjoyable act. Turning over on his belly, Matt crawled to the upper end of the pool, peering through the screening bushes in the direction from which the singing sound was coming. The light was poor. Even so, it was good enough for him to make out the figure of a girl, standing in profile not ten feet away, reaching down to the hem of her buckskin skirt, lifting it, and pulling it up over her head.

As she tossed the garment aside, she turned, momentarily facing him. His first thought was *My God, she's beautiful!* His second: *She's naked!* His third, *How can I get away from here without being seen?*

That she was not aware of his presence was made clear enough by the fact that she still was crooning her bath-taking song, her gaze intent on her footing as she stepped gingerly into a pool just a few yards upstream from the one in which he lay. Though he had stopped breathing for fear she would hear the sound, he could not justify leaving his eyes open for fear she would hear the lids closing. Morally wrong though he knew it was to stare at her, he could not even blink or look away.

She would be around sixteen years old, he judged, her skin light copper in color, her mouth wide and generous, with dimples indenting both cheeks. Her breasts were full but not heavy; her waist was slim, her stomach softly rounded, her hips beginning to broaden with maturity, her

182

legs long and graceful. Watching her sink slowly into the water until only the tips of her breasts and her head were exposed, Matt felt no guilt for continuing to stare at her. Instead he mused, *So that's what a naked woman looks like! Why should I be ashamed to admire such beauty?*

He began breathing again, careful to make no sound. Since the two pools were no more than a dozen feet apart, separated by a thin screen of bushes and a short length of stream, which here made only a faint gurgling noise, he knew that getting out of the water, retrieving his clothes and rifle, and then withdrawing from the vicinity without revealing his presence would require utmost caution. But the attempt must be made, for if one young Indian woman knew of this bathing spot, others must know of it, too, and in all likelihood soon would be coming here to join her.

He could well imagine his treatment at their hands, if found. Time and again recently the two captains had warned members of the party that Western Indians such as the Shoshones, Flatheads, and Nez Perces had a far higher standard of morality than did the Mandans, with whom the party had wintered, who would gladly sell the favor of wives and daughters for a handful of beads, a piece of bright cloth, or a cheap trade knife, and cheerfully provide shelter and bed for the act.

Moving with infinite care, he half floated, half crawled to the lower right-hand edge of the pool, where he had left his rifle and clothes. The Indian girl still was singing. The bank was steep and slick. Standing up, he took hold of a sturdy-feeling, thumb-thick sapling rooted near the edge of the bank, cautiously tested it, and judged it secure. Pulling himself out of the pool, he started to take a step, slipped, and tried to save himself by grabbing the sapling with both hands.

The full weight of his body proved too much for its root system. Torn out of the wet earth, it no longer supported him. As he fell backward into the pool, he gave an involuntary cry of disgust.

"Oh, shit!"

Underwater, his mouth, nose, and eyes filled as he struggled to turn over and regain his footing. When he did so, he immediately became aware of the fact that the girl had stopped singing. Choking, coughing up water, half-blinded, and completely disoriented, he floundered out of the pool toward where he thought his clothes and rifle were. Seeing a garment draped over a bush, he grabbed it, realized it was not his, hastily turned away, and blundered squarely into a wet, naked body.

To save themselves from falling, both he and the Indian girl clung to each other momentarily. She began screaming. Hastily he let her go. Still screaming and staring at him with terror-stricken eyes, she snatched her dress off the bush and held it so that it covered her. Finding his own clothes, he held them in front of his body, trying to calm the girl by making the sign for "friend," "white man," and "peace," while urgently saying:

"*Ta-ba-bone*, you understand? *Suyapo!* I went to sleep, you see, and had no idea you were around . . ."

Suddenly her screaming stopped. Not because of his words or hand signs, Matt feared, but because of the appearance of an Indian man who had pushed through the bushes and now stood beside her. He was dressed in beaded, fringed buckskins, was stocky, slightly bowlegged, a few inches shorter than Matt but more muscular and heavier, a man in his middle twenties, with high cheekbones and a firm jawline. He shot a guttural question at the girl, to which she replied in a rapid babble of words. His dark brown eyes blazed with anger. Drawing a glittering knife out of its sheath, he motioned the girl to step aside, and moved toward Matt menacingly.

Backing away, Mat thought frantically, *Captain Clark is not going to like this at all. And if that Indian does what it looks like he means to do with that knife, I'm not going to like it, either . . .*

A special offer for people who enjoy reading the best Westerns published today.

WESTERNS!

NO OBLIGATION

Mail the coupon below

To start your subscription and receive 2 FREE WESTERNS, fill out the coupon below and mail it today. We'll send your first shipment which includes 2 FREE BOOKS as soon as we receive it.

Mail To: **True Value Home Subscription Services, Inc. P.O. Box 5235 120 Brighton Road, Clifton, New Jersey 07015-5235**

YES! I want to start reviewing the very best Westerns being published today. Send me my first shipment of 6 Westerns for me to preview FREE for 10 days. If I decide to keep them, I'll pay for just 4 of the books at the low subscriber price of $2.75 each; a total $11.00 (a $21.00 value). Then each month I'll receive the 6 newest and best Westerns to preview Free for 10 days. If I'm not satisfied I may return them within 10 days and owe nothing. Otherwise I'll be billed at the special low subscriber rate of $2.75 each; a total of $16.50 (at least a $21.00 value) and save $4.50 off the publishers price. There are never any shipping, handling or other hidden charges. I understand I am under no obligation to purchase any number of books and I can cancel my subscription at any time, no questions asked. In any case the 2 FREE books are mine to keep.

Name _____

Street Address _____ Apt. No. _____

City _____ State _____ Zip Code _____

Telephone _____

Signature _____
(if under 18 parent or guardian must sign)

Terms and prices subject to change. Orders subject to acceptance by True Value Home Subscription Services, Inc.

10930-4